DRAGON'S FIELD

DRAGON'S FIELD

Elizabeth Gill

This first world edition published 2011
in Great Britain and in the USA by
SEVERN HOUSE PUBLISHERS LTD of
9–15 High Street, Sutton, Surrey, England, SM1 1DF.

British Library Cataloguing in Publication Data

Gill, Elizabeth, 1950-
  Dragon's field.
  1. Fishers' spouses–England–Northumberland–Fiction.
  2. Fishers–Death–Fiction. 3. Bankers–England–
  Durham–Fiction. 4. Northumberland (England)–Social
  conditions–20th century–Fiction.
  I. Title
  823.9'2-dc22

ISBN-13: 978-0-7278-8101-4 (cased)

All Severn House titles are printed on acid-free paper.

Severn House Publishers support The Forest Stewardship Council [FSC],
the leading international forest certification organisation. All our titles that
are printed on Greenpeace-approved FSC-certified paper carry the FSC logo.

Typeset by Palimpsest Book Production Ltd.,
Falkirk, Stirlingshire, Scotland.
Printed and bound in Great Britain by
MPG Books Ltd., Bodmin, Cornwall.

One

It was dark by mid-afternoon and the wind got up. It was a bitter wind, off the sea, which cut into every bared inch of her and there was not much of that, just the middle part of her face. Her hands were stuck well into the pockets of her coat. She stopped regarding the state of the weather or the feel of it against her skin after a while because none of the others complained, they just stood there listening to the tide ebbing away. Somehow it seemed worse that it should be an outgoing tide and it made a difference. An incoming tide brought the fishermen home. An outgoing tide seemed to take everything with it.

Long after darkness fell completely, long after the lights came on in the little houses beyond the beach the women stood there and others drifted down to the shore, mostly old men when their meal was finished, when their children were abed. Some of them had stood all afternoon, the women better than the men, women it seemed could be still for ever, men would shift and take their hands from their pockets because there was nothing to do but wait and they were no good at waiting.

Shona felt as though she had spent a lifetime waiting for James to come home and each night there he had been, the boat on the skyline or he would catch her unawares in good weather and be at the house before she could rush down to the beach, her hair and long skirt flying, and he would pretend to scold, saying that she was no good woman to him, that she did not look for him to come back to her. He had said that he would always come back to her. It was not a sensible thing for a fisherman, a sailor or a pitman to say, it was not, she reflected now, a sensible thing for any man to say to any woman or the other way round.

Minutes had turned into weeks and yet strangely it did not

matter. You could not move because there was no homecoming, you could not think of anything but that the boat might come into sight at any second and it would be the second when relief felt warm, when you scorned yourself for ever believing it could go wrong, just another second, then another second.

Nobody would move in case they should miss the vital second, as though if they were not there it could not happen. The boat would come into sight, the world would change. As long as you believed, everything would be all right, so the ministers said, yet they were not the ministers of the church where the fisher folk went, so James always said, because ministers in fishing villages used their words more carefully. They were not in the habit of making promises.

The other boats had come back, the first two almost on time, the next one later, the fourth a long time after that so when it made its way towards the beach the women gasped with terror and with pleasure because they did not know then whose boat it was.

More men safe, more shaken heads and silence and the downcast eyes, concentrating on pulling the coble up the beach out of the way, the waves beneath it with a kind of intake of breath noise as the shingle became firm and the water receded.

One by one, when it was quite dark, when the tide had gone all the way out and come almost all the way in so that she had had to move back to avoid getting her feet wet so many times that she had lost count, the women were persuaded to their houses by their mothers or their sisters. She had neither mother nor sister to collect her, his mother was there but did not speak, did not acknowledge her, and Shona stood long afterwards because there was nothing to go home for.

It was only when she had retreated as far back as the soft sand at the top of the beach that she heard a movement behind her and knew it for Collum's tread that she turned around and saw his shadow. There was no moon but she would have known his form anywhere, tall and slender as James was, but he stood as though he was not welcome, a hesitancy about him somehow, he had always looked as though he belonged somewhere else and had just happened in, it was what they had in common, she thought.

He and James had had a boat together once and then they had quarrelled when James had brought her to the village.

They had not spoken since. Collum had got his own boat. James had called him 'that ignorant bloody mick' which was both insulting and inaccurate since Collum's family had been settled there for generations and were Methodists, and hired another man in his place but always she felt there was room in the boat where Collum should have been and James was aware of it.

When he stood in the boat he moved around Collum's invisible presence. They had been boys together. She was sorry she had come between them, not least because she often saw him in the street and he looked and smiled though never spoke of course, nobody spoke to her, and there was about his look a longing so that she knew he liked, even admired, her and was remembering what they had all been and were no longer and none of it could be retrieved.

'He's lost, you know it,' Collum said now, his voice as unsteady as the waves just below her feet.

She said nothing.

'Come back up then, eh?'

James had called his boat 'Rainbow's Girl' as though she and the boat were in direct competition, as if the boat had somehow won and the boat was a bigger whore than any woman had been and was her enemy, she had known from the beginning. She had wished she could ever have asked him to do a safer job, a different one, but you didn't fall in love with a fisherman and then wish he was a landsman. It would have made him laugh and she was too proud to tell him that she feared for him each time he went out, that she had never got used to what he did, that the waiting was hard. Now it would never end. The boat and the sea had won.

The morning of the funeral she looked around her tidy little house and could not bear to think of it without him. He was never coming back and she did not know what to do. Nobody would take her in, she had no friends, she had hoped one day that they would move to some other place where they would be better received but she had known always that he would never go, this was where the sea called him. The boat and the men in the boat who did not even socialize with him now and the sea were his whole life beyond her and she had stood it because of him even though so many times it had been impossible.

Before she left the house some instinct made her go into the bedroom and take every penny that she had and stuff it into her purse, the savings that she had accumulated over the years. She felt insecure now as never before and wanted the money on her for the comfort. She could trust no one. She did not honestly think anyone would come into her house, they would all be at the funeral and their minds were on the tragedy which had befallen them, but somehow she was unwilling to go anywhere and leave the money behind so she took it and put her purse and James's wallet deep into her coat pocket beneath her gloves.

Shona understood at least a little why in some places it was fitting only for the men to go to the funerals while women busied themselves with teacups and children and food, but she had no place among the women here either. She thought she would never eat again, would never feel anything beyond this ghastly loss.

She was the only woman. The men ignored her. She didn't mind, she was there for James. She stood apart now, walked right down to the front of the little church, she didn't even have to make herself do it, it came naturally to her, where the coffins stood at the front.

It was her right, she felt, she didn't care what their customs were, she had never been one of them anyway, she had nothing to lose. There was silence, no organ played in such a place, it was the plainest church that she had ever seen, whitewashed inside and stone built without, and it had housed the funeral of many a fisherman before this.

James had not been inside that church since he had brought Shona back to the village so many years ago and sometimes he would say that it didn't matter, he knew his God.

He must know his God a lot better by now, Shona thought with a sigh as she sat down in the front pew and watched the coffins, she sang the hymns which had been chosen by other people, listened to the minister talking about the men in glowing ways such as nobody had ever done before and she put her head down when the tears threatened.

The church stood at the head of the bay and the churchyard beyond it and this was where the procession with the coffins went after the service. She walked, away from the men, into the bright sunshine of the autumn morning and watched from beneath the trees. It was a surprisingly warm October day, warmer than many of the summer days had been, and a mild breeze blew there up on the hillside. From there she could see the sea so blue and the sky paler and little white clouds far up.

Buried in sight of their loved and hated water were master mariners and fishermen, their wives, their daughters and their sons, some of them old, some of them children and many of them like this, drowned at sea. Beyond and below was the village, the little rooftops glistening in the sunshine and the sand dunes and the tall green spiky grass and the little ways to the beach made by the constant feet of children over the years so that they could jump on to the beach, watch from there for the boats coming home.

It was a busy funeral, the men were so well known, people came from miles around and those who could not get into the church lined the streets and stood there with bowed heads as though it helped and it did, she pictured it afterwards as she made her way home.

She expected to be alone at the cottage, none of her neighbours would call. She was still the outsider, even after fifteen years. She had been back inside but a few minutes when the door opened and James's brother strode into her house in a way in which he had never done before. He had with him one of his friends, another fisherman, she couldn't remember his name.

'Ma wants her furniture,' his brother said.

She stood staring at him and without any further conversation he propped open the door with one of her kitchen chairs and went into the living room and came back with an ornate little table.

'You can't take that.'

He ignored her and continued carrying it outside and she

ran after him and got in his way so that he stopped. He walked
around her and when she got in the way again he merely
pushed her aside and loaded the little table, flat side down, on
a large cart.

'You have no right.'

'Don't get in my road,' and when she did he pushed her
aside again so brusquely that she fell against the cart and hurt
her hip.

She got up and went back inside, thinking only that she
had knives in her kitchen drawer and that she had to stop him
somehow but she was just in time to see the other man empty
the contents of her kitchen drawers into a big sack and when
she shouted at him he merely grinned.

'Any time you want a man, love, you know where I am,'
he said. 'You'll be gasping for it in a week, the sort of lass you
are.'

She recognized him, married with four small children, and
she could smell beer on his breath and his teeth were dirty
and gapped and she backed away then, afraid.

They loaded up the furniture on the cart and it was more
than she could bear to object further, she stood there, dumb,
watching.

They even took the bedclothes, including a quilt in blue
and yellow which she and James had bought in Alnwick on a
special day away. They took the china from the cupboards and
pans from the stove. When they had finished there was nothing
left to sit on except a small stool.

Jack smiled, looking about him to make sure he had cleared
the place. At the door was a mat which she used to prevent
mud and dirt from getting into the house. He even lifted that
and as he swept out of the house and banged the door something fell from the underside of it. He didn't look back so he
didn't see it, but then it was only a letter.

When she had closed the door behind the two men there
was nothing to do but go and pick it up. She listened as the
cart trundled away with almost everything she possessed.

She stood, wondering what on earth she was going to do
now. There was not sufficient wood to make a fire and the
bright October afternoon was fast descending into darkness.

Usually she loved these times, James would be coming home to her, she would be preparing a meal, the fire would be blazing up and she had enjoyed night wrapping its fingers around the little village as the lamps were lit and all was quiet.

She remembered the letter. They got very few, there was no need, nothing which was of the world concerned them beyond the village. She went across and picked it up and it was very official-looking so that it scared her but then everything that could go wrong, even her own comfort and safety, had gone so what was there to be afraid of?

She was suddenly very weary, had there been a bed to sleep in she thought she would have taken off the outer layer of her clothes and sunk beyond the lovely blue and yellow quilt.

The letter was cream and oblong and the paper was thick. She pulled out the single sheet inside. It was from a solicitors', Hedley, Jameson and Hedley, and there was an address in Durham City.

But what worried her more than the fact that these people were solicitors – she had never had anything to do with solicitors before and she felt the sudden draught of James's absence – was the date on the headed letter, it was February 10th. She felt a flash of guilt over her own shoddy housekeeping for however many times she had swept around the mat and even sometimes under it she felt sure and she had lifted it and taken it out and banged it against the wall a dozen times and more – this had somehow been there all that time.

She read on and then she went over and sat down on the little stool and she looked through the words again to make sense of them.

The letter was to inform her that her father had died and Mr Hedley would be glad if she would call at his office at her earliest convenience. 'Earliest' made her smile involuntarily and she felt guilt again. She had felt so many different sorts of guilt lately that she didn't mind somehow. It was just another reason to make her feel worse.

She sat there for so long that the room became dark and then, going about picking up her clothes in the bedroom, there was nothing much left, just a few items which Jack had discarded, she took the one bag she had and folded them into it and then she put on her coat, put the letter safely inside the bag and ventured outside.

The wind almost took her breath away. It was a bitterly cold night now and clear and so many stars twinkling above her that it was unseemly somehow for the sky to be so beautiful and then she remembered James lying in a cold patch of earth and she hurried along three doors to where Collum and his family lived and she banged on the door.

His mother opened it. They had not met that day because Ida, like the other village women, had not gone to the funeral and would know now full well that Shona had broken yet another rule and gone to the church with the men.

'Could I – could I speak with Collum?' She needed somebody to talk to so badly.

Ida closed the door and came outside.

'I'm afraid you cannot,' she said.

'Is he not at home?'

Ida looked sorry for her for a moment or two and then her eyes hardened.

'You have nothing to do with my son, Shona, and I'm glad of it. I knew no good would come of it when James brought a lass here from some other place and now look.'

Shona stared. What could she mean?

'The only time I have seen Collum was when he came down to the beach that day.' She couldn't go on. 'That day' had been the worst of her life. 'I just need some help. I need—'

'This is all your fault,' Ida said and then Shona understood and was horrified.

They were blaming her for what had happened. It must be somebody's fault, it always was, and they could not take it out on the sea, the October tides, the waves which at this season of the year spread and crashed up the beach like avenging animals.

'Can I come inside just for a few moments?'

'We can't afford to have James's family involving us in what has happened. They never liked you and after what you have done nobody will take you in. You have a home to go to presumably. Go to it. You have no place here. Your cottage will be given to Robbie Arnison, God knows he's waited long enough for one,' and she closed the door.

Shona struggled against the wind, back down the row and inside the shelter of the cottage where she and James had been so happy and where now there was nothing left. She had not even the means of making a cup of tea.

She sat by the window on the little stool, wrapped in her coat with her bag and purse beside her, and waited for dawn. It would be a long time but since James had died she had not slept or eaten, just made endless cups of tea and watched the day give way to night and the night to day.

Two

It had been January when the man had collapsed outside Darling's bank in the Market Place of Durham City. Harry had been in his office and Miss Piers, his secretary, had rushed through with nothing more than, 'Oh come quickly, Mr Darling, somebody's hurt.'

As though he could be in the least bit useful where people and their ailments were concerned, Harry thought impatiently as he ran through the wide hall of the building and out into the bitter wind.

He silently cursed Miss Piers for coming straight to him instead of giving the message to any one of half a dozen employees she must have had to pass on her way but then that was Miss Piers for you, she probably thought he had control over these things, and then he saw the crowd beginning to gather. Incidents like this had happened before, it was as if people got almost to his door for succour and then their courage failed them and they could not approach him for help.

Sometimes he felt that people thought of him like the sanctuary knocker on the door of the cathedral, that if they got as far as his bank everything would be all right and they could breathe for a time. Sometimes, they were right. This time however the man had not been so fortunate.

He died even as Harry bent over him, without a word, without another breath, and Harry had a desire to take the man up from the pavement so that he would not die on the cold stone where a few thick square flakes of snow were already beginning to fall with perfect and appalling timing. The pavement was wet, the man had possibly slipped and hit his head but there was no blood. Harry did not want him to die alone but he had already done so, oblivious to the curious crowd who hovered above him, forming a circle just a little

way back because they did not really want to be involved, all
they wanted was to go home to their neighbours and recount
the incident and no doubt tell of the bank manager kneeling
in the wet street – ruining his good suit, Harry thought, but
nobody else would care.

He felt instantly bereft as though there was something more
he could have done, as though he could have attempted rescue,
used the magic which folk thought doctors and solicitors and
even bank managers somehow had to improve their lives, their
poverty, their failing businesses, the grimness of the back streets,
the lack of work, the awful labour which was offered them.
It was not much of a life, he thought, for most people.
Sometimes, he thought grimly, the doctor could help in circumstances like these but the man was beyond it.

He stayed there until the doctor came, a little Scotsman
called Menzies who proclaimed that the man was dead and
then they carried the body into a back room behind the closed
doors of the bank. Luckily Miss Piers had had the sense to
remove the people who were waiting to see him from the
reception into another room so the place was deserted. Even
the clerks had gone. They were probably glad of his absence
so that they could make tea and eat biscuits and talk.

'Know him?' Menzies said when they were alone.

Harry shook his head and then looked closer and realized
that he did and it was a shock and he went on staring but the
doctor was already closing his bag, muttering about undertakers
and the cost to the local authority and he was gone in moments
to his next case.

Harry tried to go back to work but he couldn't concentrate.
He sat at his desk all the way through his dinner hour at
midday which he never took, unlike his employees who came
and went to and from the building at various times, chatting and
laughing, and he envied them their friendliness. He sat well
into the afternoon as the winter day closed in around him and
soft snow began to fall once more beyond his window.

When it was completely dark but not late, only about three
o'clock, he told Miss Piers that he was going out. She looked
rather surprised because she knew everywhere he went and
everything he did during the day and never enquired as to

what he did the rest of the time. It would have been an intrusion and Harry permitted no one into his private life but he had no meeting arranged for that afternoon.

She merely nodded and told him to remember his gloves because the day was bitter, she had been out at dinner time, no doubt having a hot pie in the Silver Street cafe with one of her colleagues. Miss Piers was a great miss to mothering, Harry thought affectionately as he went.

He put on his heavy coat, hat and gloves and when it was such a dark afternoon that people were barely recognizable he left the wide cobbled market square where he had made his living for the past fourteen years and walked the short distance down the hill towards Elvet Bridge and down the narrow steep steps which led to the river and from there beyond Brown's Boathouse he stepped into another world.

He could not believe that it was such a short distance between the two places because it had taken every bit of courage he possessed to go back, everything he was capable of to cover that distance from all those years ago and all the will and patience and guts that he could summon to become the person that he was now and leave it behind.

The feelings came running back, the sounds and sights and smells of his early life came upon him more thickly than the snow which was now falling fast and turning everything white in the darkness and it was a relief to have a covering because the place where he went now was known as Paradise Lane and it was enough to make even a cynical man such as he had become smile a little.

It was a hell-hole, it was a shameful thing that a city which boasted some of the most beautiful buildings in the world, where the Church was prosperous on the backs of its people, such places as this were tolerated. Harry had not voluntarily set foot inside a church in years and would not, despite how apparently respectable he had become.

He was rich and eligible, every mother in town offered him a place at her dinner parties, everybody wanted to know him.

He had been raised in much worse places than this, had had a harder life than here in a narrow back street, a place where there was never any peace, silence or comfort, never enough to eat and no love of any kind but then he had found Shona Hardy and Paradise Lane had been worthy of its name after that.

It seemed fitting somehow that Shona's father, Tam, had died in front of his bank. It was like the old man had planned it, was glad to expire in his rags, in his dirt outside Harry's gleaming spotless place of business. It was flawless, he made sure it was, and everybody who worked for him knew that he would settle for nothing less than perfection.

It was the very opposite of the place where he stood now, the houses cramped one against another as though leaning together was the only way they could stay up. There was nobody on the street as there would have been had it been fine but he knew very well that the little houses were freezing in winter because they were falling apart and airless in summer because they were crowded together.

He knew that at night the creatures came on to the floors and into the beds, he knew that damp and mould encouraged them and the unwashed bodies provided homes for fleas and lice, that silverfish slithered on the floor and slimy beings dropped on you while you slept. Harry could hardly stand up within minutes, he felt so faint but he would not lean against anything here, and it was not just the wet and the cold it was the invisible stain which would not come off.

Shona Hardy had rescued him from these things, her house had been clean and welcoming, he could hardly bear to come here now because he could remember her voice, her laughter.

She had been kind, better than that, she would not turn away even from a sparrow with a bent wing, she could not help herself, giving to those in need, he remembered her on the market, slipping pennies to small boys, selling curtains cheaply to women who had little, rescuing even the very air from responsibility. Every day to Shona could be good, everything could be helped by rest and food and her brusque enquiries which she sought so hard not to soften.

She was the reason he did not want to come back here, the memories of her kindness were harder than all the memories of his life.

The snow dulled the sounds from the houses, muffled the

noise of his feet, and he was glad that the place was empty because somebody might recognize him, might bridge the gap which had been partly closed today when the old man had died in front of him. He had fought against the instinct which brought him there but he didn't fight any more now.

He walked, he could have found the house with his eyes closed so the darkness was no problem to him. The door wasn't even shut, why would it be, there was nothing for anyone to steal, and when he pushed it open and it creaked a little he felt sick because he was nothing but a grubby child and Tam Hardy was saying, 'Howay in, lad,' as he never had even when he was drunk and when Harry got inside Shona would be seeing to the fire and because of her it had been a better place. She made fires and dinners, and people called her 'bonny lass' and it was always true. Somehow Shona was something special with her bright orange hair, the same colour as marmalade, and warm blue eyes like a fire lit inside them.

Harry paused now in the doorway, quietening the memories until he could hear nothing but the river below, tumbling its way to the coast because there had been so much rain, sleet and snow. It had frozen last week, the water stilled and strange and the ducks and seagulls paddling across the top, bemused by the situation. The icicles had hung for days on the ends of the buildings and slowly dripped their way to extinction.

He didn't want to make a light in case anybody noticed but in the end he couldn't see well enough to find what he had come for and he spied the lamp and lit it and it filled the room with shadows. It was a poor room, it hadn't changed in all those years. One room with a pantry on the end and another which was a sitting room and upstairs two bedrooms and between them a narrow staircase with its tiny landing.

There was a table but nothing on it and two chairs and there was a settee over by the wall which had long since become home to rats, he could hear something scurrying away from the light. In the corner there was the black gap of under the stairs hidden by a curtain. He didn't want to investigate in there but he had no choice so he took the lamp over. There was nothing but dust. The other room was empty as though nobody had used it for years.

He took the lamp up the stairs, half expecting that the time would change and he would be twelve or thirteen again but nothing happened and he turned into the bigger of the two bedrooms and here was the double bed which had always been there. There were sheets and blankets and if they had been washed in the past few years they certainly didn't look it, the whole thing in a heap and further over was a chest of drawers. He put down the lamp and opened the drawers but they were empty.

He investigated the other room but it held nothing at all, not even the narrow beds where he and Shona had slept all those years ago. He was just about to go back downstairs when he noticed the cut along the floorboard and how slightly unevenly it had been laid back down and he put the lamp on the floor and got his gloved hands to work on it for a few moments and then it gave.

If he had been looking for money he would have been disappointed but then he knew Tam Hardy too well, there would be nothing of that sort of value, it was something quite different he was looking for, a thick folded paper perhaps even in an envelope. His soft leather-bound fingers closed around it and with a small sigh of satisfaction he drew it away from the floor and towards the light.

He carried the lamp downstairs and gazed at the paper just sufficiently so that he knew what it was and then he placed the paper in his coat pocket and shut off the light and put it down in the middle of the table and then he left the house, closing the door as best he could behind it, it had swollen so much with the rains over time and no longer fitted its allotted space.

He walked by the river in the darkness, under Elvet Bridge and up beyond to where the banks swept to the cathedral, the castle, the square of grass which was Palace Green and all the places around it which were owned by the Church or the University and came around the loop in the river which had so long ago made Durham so difficult for intruders to reach, so easy to defend, and then he walked along past the old fulling mill and finally up onto Framwellgate Bridge, not pausing to see the famous view of the castle and cathedral, he rarely looked at it, and then he made his way slowly up the cobbled winding Silver Street until he gained the Market Place once again.

There were shops and businesses flourishing around the edge of the market and in the far corner St Nicholas's Church stood with its spire, the road led out and up to Claypath and away to the east beyond the city but Harry went no further and was glad to reach the warmth of his office.

He was in there only moments before Miss Piers came in with a tray and on it was a silver teapot, sugar basin and milk jug, in it was his favourite Ceylon tea and with it several neatly triangular sandwiches. She did this every day at five because he didn't go home. His staff went at half-past five and Miss Piers, though she would have stayed until he left, went before six and he always had to tell her to go and there he would sit during the evening, sometimes working and sometimes not, watching the darkness of the countryside.

This room was private for him and for his clients, nobody must know they were there, bank business was for each person and Harry had made his fortress secure from the bottom to the top. There was no one who could contradict him, nobody who would dare, he chose his people carefully, if they spoke about the bank outside of it he had them dismissed. He paid them well and expected their loyalty and many of them had worked for him for ten years or more.

He knew all about each one of them, their families and their lives, but many of them knew nothing about him other than that he had worked his way up to this, owned the bank, and were assured of their employment so long as they did what was required of them and you couldn't say that of most businesses, Harry knew.

He was careful, he allotted them jobs which were often a little beyond them but not too much so that they would retain ambition and not be bored, feel good about themselves because they could see the progress they made and if they failed he did not tell them but got somebody else to help so that they would see where they were going. He had made one or two mistakes but mostly they were good honest hard-working

people and they knew that they could go on to be bank
manager in one of the other towns.

Harry had put young men with families into many banks
in the area, giving them a house so that they could see their
growing children and paying them so that they would be
satisfied and not worry about money and do their jobs well
in the small communities, getting to know everyone and going
home at night pleased with their day's work to a good dinner
and their children in bed. It was part fantasy, he was sure this
rarely happened, but it had been his dream and he tried to
maintain it.

Miss Piers put out the beef sandwiches for him with a snowy
white napkin on a plate and resting on it she placed a silver
knife. She poured out his tea and when he sat back and took
the cup and saucer she sat down in the chair across his desk
and as usual began to work her way through his next day's
appointments and then the invitations which had arrived.

'There are dinner invitations from Mr and Mrs Hobson,
that's Mr Oscar—'

'No.'

'And from Mr and Mrs Clements—'

'No.'

They went through this daily. Miss Piers tried not to sigh.

'There is the dedication of the window—'

'No.'

'And the wedding of—'

'No.'

She looked at him.

'And there were a great many cards this morning which I
would have put on your desk—'

'No.'

'Do you wish them to be sent to your hotel?'

'No, I don't.'

She looked helplessly at him.

'It's your birthday,' she said.

'How on earth people know I have no idea. Thank you,
Daisy, I am aware of it.'

He very rarely called her Daisy. Miss Piers blushed in
acknowledgement of the compliment and he thought how

very important she was to him. He couldn't run this place without her. It had been her birthday in December and he had bought her diamond ear rings, large and not quite vulgar but big enough so that they should wink and blink and make every woman who observed them envious. They had cost him a great deal and he was glad to give them to her and she had stared at them. Miss Piers was fifty-five and he felt sure that no man had ever bought her diamond ear rings before.

'Oh, Mr Darling, it's too much.'

'No,' he said, 'it's not nearly enough.'

When he had discovered her as a lowly clerk, living with her mother in a terraced house which shook when the trains went over the viaduct at the north end of the city, he had realized how intelligent this woman was. To the world she was his secretary but she had very good organizational skills.

When he went to the branches she went with him and she knew everything about the employees, how much money each branch made and what could be done to improve it, and when they were alone in the back of his car she would voice her opinions as she had done to no one else, nor had the opportunity of doing so, he thought. He had bought her a house the year before, a pretty house in Hallgarth Street, brick and still terraced but substantial, and this had brought tears to her eyes.

'You're very kind,' she had said.

'You save me a great deal of money, a lot of sweat and temper, and I want you to know it.'

'Will there be anything else, Mr Darling?' she said now.

'Yes, I want to see Aidan Hedley, preferably tomorrow.'

'I will arrange it.'

The following morning he saw the solicitor, Aidan Hedley. Aidan was the kind of man that Harry had wanted to be. Aidan's business had been his father's and his grandfather's. He was well respected in town and came from a comfortable middle-class family. He had gone to a minor public school and then to Oxford. He was confident and clearly spoken and everybody admired him.

Harry could have hated Aidan Hedley but he admired ability

in other men and Aidan had a great deal of ability. He was the best lawyer in the area, if he hadn't been Harry wouldn't have employed him, and also Harry rather liked him because he had no what the local people called 'set off'. He was to marry a woman who had created a huge scandal. Aidan, Harry thought with pleasure, had not even put a hair out of place either while she did it or since.

He admired it in Aidan. Aidan's firm and name had weathered it because Aidan was so well liked and so good at what he did. His father and Mr Jameson had helped people who needed it, Harry knew by now, those who could not pay, and Aidan did the same and he needed clients like Harry who paid well in order to carry on his business.

'What can I help you with?' Aidan asked when they had shaken hands and the Assam tea had arrived straight away in white fluted thin china cups and they had sat down on chairs which were so comfortable that visitors were mostly reluctant to leave.

There was also the view which looked out towards the countryside, it took in the railway line, the passing trains, the beginning of fields which led to various farms between here and the next towns but Harry was used to the view and didn't regard it.

He handed the will over to Aidan and said simply, 'He died yesterday out the front there.'

'I heard about it.'

Aidan, thought Harry, was a good solicitor, knew everything that went on in his town.

'I didn't realize it was Tam Hardy,' Aidan said. 'What do you know about him?'

'Nothing much,' Harry lied.

Aidan scanned the paper.

'Is this the only copy?'

'As far as I know.'

'Do you know where the daughter is?'

'Not exactly.'

Aidan looked carefully at him as though he would have liked a better answer and he waited and in the end Harry gave it to him.

'She married. He was a fisherman. He came from some village in Northumberland.'

Aidan looked slightly pained, there were so many fishing villages in Northumberland and a great many fishermen.

'She and her father were completely estranged, hadn't spoken in fifteen years as far as I'm aware.'

'And you had the will?'

It was a polite way of not asking the direct question, Harry thought. Neat.

'I went to Paradise Lane, to his home, and found it. I'll pay for the funeral so make sure he has a decent coffin, a good stone and whatever else is needed. Don't stint on it.'

Aidan said nothing and Harry heard all the other unasked questions, like why had he gone there instead of sending somebody else, why had he bothered, what interest could he possibly have now and what did he know about Shona Hardy?

It was just as well he didn't ask them, though Harry had known he wouldn't, Aidan was far too much the solicitor to make mistakes like that but it was only now that Harry thought of how he had gone back there when he had no need and there was nothing in it for him and yet he had risked the dirt and the fleas and the possibility of being robbed, at least Aidan would think that. Nobody in Paradise Lane would have touched Harry Darling, he was as safe there as he was at the Royal County Hotel where he lived in Old Elvet.

'Do you know her husband's name?'

'He was called James Rainbow,' Harry said.

Three

There was only the one memory or perhaps it was a hundred memories all running into one another, of her mother lying in bed downstairs in the kitchen of the house in Paradise Lane. It was a sick room and the smells were of medicine and camphor and she could see her father sitting on the bed and bathing her mother's face and holding her in his arms and all Shona had wanted was some attention.

Nobody fed her. She was obliged to eat heels of bread in the pantry with the door closed to try to shut out her mother's pain. She remembered the steep stairs, the shadows and the movement of them in the almost darkness and the silence there with no light to go to bed.

Sometimes when her mother was quiet she would prompt him and Shona would go to the shop on the corner for food. No cooking was done, it had to be something you could eat straight from the packet, fish and chips, pies and peas. The times like this were fewer and fewer as her mother sweated and groaned and her father called on God not to take his wife and Shona began to wish that he would and swiftly, it seemed to her that the pain was beyond bearing and yet her mother had to endure it and Shona had to listen to her.

It was summer with no fire in the grate, the door open for any vestige of breeze that might waft in from the river. The house was stifling and her father continued to sponge her mother's body with cold cloths, all that seemed to ease her.

Shona was not allowed to go beyond the door, her father feared she would drown, he said. She wanted just to go as far as the street, she could hear other children playing and chanting the songs of skipping and hopscotch from outside. She was too shy to join in and from the safety of knowing she could not go she longed to be with them, to be a part of anything which was not to do with how ill her mother was.

And then it was over and after that as the cold autumn set in her father did not notice her any more than he had. The bed was taken from the kitchen back upstairs and sometimes her father even went up there to sleep but to Shona the bed was still there in the kitchen and a hundred times a day she would look at the space and wonder where her mother was now and indeed her father because after the noise and the sweating had stopped her mother lay lifeless in her father's arms while he cried.

They both left in a way, her mother for whatever was beyond the graveyard and her father for some pub. The house was so silent that Shona could hear the rain on the towpath beyond, thought she could even hear the rain falling into the river.

That autumn it rained so much that the river and the bank sides were grey for weeks on end and the birds which usually lived around the place were obliged to try to find food elsewhere because the river was foam-flecked and too swift for them to catch any fish or find anything edible below the surface. It rushed past in brown torrents on days when the fog lifted.

The money in the jug on the kitchen mantelpiece ran out and so did the money in her father's pockets and he was obliged to go back to work. He would leave her alone in the house without food or heat so in the end she went with him. She did not know how it had happened, he did not ask her to go, and the markets where he made his living were as uncomfortable as their home, out there in all weathers and sometimes with no top sheets if they were in scarce supply or the market man in charge would not give you them unless you paid him extra and her father had little enough money and sometimes could not afford to do this and it was always on rainy days.

As she got older Shona became wily. She stole money from the back of the stall or from his pockets when he slept. She went back in the evenings and lit the kitchen fire which she laid before she went out every morning. She washed clothes in the sink in the pantry and if the day was fine she would sling them across a line in the back lane as she saw her neighbours do. If the day was wet she would group them on the clothes horse around the fire but that made her miserable in the evenings because she would be there alone and all the heat was taken by the steaming clothes and the house was cold and damp and she could not escape.

Her father did not talk to her, he did not help her to do anything in their daily lives, not on purpose, she thought, but as though he was almost totally unaware of his own existence and not at all of hers.

If food was put in front of him he ate it, if not he didn't seem to notice. Very often he did not get out of bed, he could not be relied on to go to work but if he had any money he would go out and in some ways she had learned to be glad when he did not make much money because she secreted what she found and he could not drink it away in the nearest pub. He would go to bed and leave her over the fire and she would take comfort in that and in the fish and chips she would go out for. Fish and chips hot, with vinegar and salt, was the best dinner of all.

Four

In Paradise Lane you did not stop in the dark for any reason so it was lucky that the still form was almost outside their door, Shona Hardy thought. Her father would have left it there in the freezing night but she could not. The weather was bitter and had frozen, the body was covered in snow. After she and her father had gone inside she brought out the lamp she had lit and saw that the person on their doorstep was a young boy, about her own age, perhaps twelve or thirteen. She could not lift him by herself, so, having brushed the snow away from his face, she went in and told her father but he would not help.

'He could die or could be already dead just outside.'

'It's nothing to do with me,' her father said and he took his candle and went upstairs to bed.

She went back outside once again. She was afraid that it was a corpse and did not want to touch it for fear he was already cold but when she put the back of her fingers to his face there was a lingering warmth. She called into his ear.

'You must get up.'

When there was no response she tried shaking him. His clothes were thin and already the snow had frozen against them again. She continued to shake his shoulder and shout and after what seemed to her like a very long time he opened his eyes.

'You must get up,' she said again.

He hesitated for a few moments longer, focused, looked at her and then when she said it again for perhaps the tenth time he got to his feet, very slowly, and he was taller than she had thought. She did not have to wait for him to follow her into the house, though it was not much better inside. She had not stopped to light the fire. He shivered and she thought that was a good thing, it meant he was getting warmer. She lit the fire. Her father had not really gone to bed, he had just retreated so that he did not have to become involved. He was a great one for not becoming involved in anything, he had had enough long since, he told her, he did not care any more.

'Here.' She beckoned the boy towards a chair by the fire and after a moment or two he took it, holding his hands up to the blaze as she lit another lamp.

She had left the remains of a stew from the day before. With bread which she had bought earlier from Doris from the indoor market and hastily sliced all of it, there was sufficient for three people. She heated it over the fire and the smell of it brought her father downstairs. He said nothing but sat himself at the table and she waved at the boy and he sat down too and she ladled the stew, steam rising from it on to the plates she had warmed in the oven, and she made tea and then her father, who had not spoken, went off to bed.

The question was in the boy's eyes and she had been considering it all the way through the meal – ever since the moment she had taken the responsibility upon herself to do something to try and help.

Should she let him stay? What if he stole? What if he was a weird one and came to her in the night and touched and demanded her body? What if he murdered her and her father – she was amused at the idea that her father had been only a second thought. But she did not turn him away, the night was bitter and he might die. She went upstairs and found blankets in the cupboard and on the tiny landing and she gave him one of her pillows and she took them downstairs. She indicated the other room and then he spoke for the first time. His voice was throaty as though it wasn't used much.

'Can I stay by the fire, miss?'

It was as if she had offered him the greatest luxury of all when she nodded.

'There will be a draught,' she said and then remembered that he had been unconscious in the snow. She put down the pillow and the blankets on the rug by the fire.

'If you need the – lav, it's down the yard,' she said and he nodded. 'If you go out make sure you lock the door when you come back.'

'Yes, miss.'

'It's Shona.'

'Shona.'

He looked at her in a way that nobody ever had before and it was because, she could see, that she meant he would lock the door against the world while he was inside. It was a very big thing for her to do, she didn't know him, couldn't trust him really. He looked so clearly at her from eyes so brown that they were almost black.

He settled himself by the fire like a tired dog and moments later he was asleep.

Shona lay in her bed listening for sounds, discounting the shouts from the street beyond, the laughter and the drunken conversation as the men turned out into the night. She heard music too though distant, somebody playing a mouth organ, it sounded so wistful in the cold starlit night, like a dying soul and then her thoughts drifted away. Nobody attacked her in her bed.

Through the wall she could hear her father snoring and he did not care, he had never cared for anything she thought, after her mother had died, but from downstairs there was nothing but silence and she imagined the boy's even breathing and the fire dying slowly and the room growing cold.

Would he notice it and turn over? Would he think he was still outside, unable to distinguish cold from warmth because he was too far gone? She didn't think so, not now that she had rescued him. His stomach was full and he had comfort and he should sleep. It troubled her, what she had done, but how could she have left him out there?

What if he had died – and that was when she realized that it was not for him that she had done it but for her own peace of mind, for herself. She turned over towards the wall, which was how she always finally put her thoughts to rest, and she knew she would go to sleep because at this time, in this posture, she always did.

The following day her father did not remark upon the fact that the boy was still there. They ate breakfast, the boy did not speak but wolfed down his bread and jam and black tea and followed them to the market, though nobody asked him to. Shona half hoped he would go away and cause her no further concern, he was like a puppy or a kitten that you could not abandon and had nowhere to go but he was rather tall and took up a great deal of the space in the house somehow.

She didn't know what to do or what to think but it appeared to her that he had worked on markets before. It rained and he was the first to ensure that the tarpaulin did not slip down and empty the gathered water on to the unsuspecting customers. He was good at keeping dry and at keeping the items for sale dry.

Her father was at that time selling shawls and scarves, brooches and hat pins, things which could be stolen. The cheapest things were always at the front of the stall so that if small thieving fingers reached for them without Shona or her father realizing it the loss would not be great but the boy had eyes so good that nobody got away with anything, he even ran after one urchin and retrieved the glass and gilt brooch which had been grabbed.

Shona was a little sorrowful, the child had been so thin and so badly dressed that she did not know whether it was a boy or a girl, but she needed every penny, she could not care for them all though she would help when she could. Her father had turned approving eyes on the boy who was helping them. Also while she watched that morning the boy spoke for the first time that day and it was to a customer, a middle-aged woman who hovered in front of the stall.

'You won't see owt any other place like that, missus. It come straight from the Orient, that did.'

The woman laughed and told him to get away but indeed it did look as though it had come from some spectacular and wonderful place. She always worried about what her father bought, his taste was indiscriminate and there were two big boxes of these long trailing scarves which he had got from a black man with a gold ear ring who spoke little English, the week before, behind the Three Tuns in Elvet.

They were raspberry coloured scarves with tiny gold threads, or purple with black and silver, or yellow with gold. She could imagine them moving in the wind but she had doubted that the women of Durham would buy them. They had no money for such fripperies, many of them had scarcely sufficient for necessities.

The reason her father was so bad as a stall holder was that he lacked imagination, she thought. He did not understand that people would buy only what they needed unless you could talk them into it. The woman now looked at the boy and then he grinned and his dirty face was lit by his clear brown eyes. He was transformed. He held up the scarf and passed it through his fingers as though it was treasure and just at that moment the sun came out and the purple and silver scarf picked up the sun's rays and glinted.

The boy did a little dance, coming around by the side of the stall to the front and picking up the notes of where the old bearded man was playing the Northumbrian pipes just across the market square.

He was playing the song which she did not know the name of but which stayed in her memory about the lovers on either side of the Tyne and the boatman who would perhaps ferry one of them over to the other. It haunted her because somehow it seemed as if he never would, as though the waters of the Tyne came between them for ever and they would look but never touch.

As he went on playing the boy went on dancing, his feet lifted and light as though he had forgotten that he had lain outside the night before in the snow, as though he had no trouble to remember. The woman started to laugh, a crowd gathered and people clapped and cheered. The woman bought the scarf for more than the price intended, for what the boy asked her.

Other women bought scarves. Shona felt slightly guilty that they should be taken in in such a way, remembering how little her father had bought the scarves for. The black man had been desperate to sell them yet it was magic and perhaps they would always feel the magic in their so dearly bought possession, would remember the bright snowy day, the sound of the pipes and the boy's feet, lifted in intricate pattern.

That afternoon the boy danced around the stall time after time and the old man who played the pipes, eager to sense an opportunity, played on just beyond the market.

When the scarves were all gone the boy put a shawl around his shoulders and did a perfect imitation of a woman who could not make up her mind whether to buy or not and there was much laughter and the air around the stall seemed to Shona to rain with pennies, threepenny bits and silver sixpences.

For the first time ever she and her father were obliged to go home early because there was nothing left to pack and take home with them, nothing left to sell. She gave the man who had played the pipes what she thought was a decent share and he thanked her and went off.

On the way back she stopped and bought pies and peas and then they went home and she lit the fire. She was left there with the boy, her father had gone with the rest of the takings and would be at the pub until there was nothing left. She and the boy ate their supper over the fire, she could see, beyond the dirt, his lean and pale face cream and slender and unmarked in the firelight. As they were drinking their black tea he spoke for the first time since they had reached home.

'Have you things to sell tomorrow?' he said.

She nodded and then put down her tea cup and took up the lamp and led him into the other room where the things her father had been unable to sell were piled high, ugly ornaments in garish colours, rugs so thin that nobody had wanted them, blankets and cardigans and socks and brown jugs and black-and-white vases, thin summer dresses and thick woollen stockings.

He began to sort out the good garments into piles and he selected what he obviously thought would sell the following day and she brought another lamp and lit it and between them they tied string around what they had chosen, ready to put them on to the cart. When this was done she took water from the boiler, gave him a thin towel and a bowl and soap and a flannel and she said, 'Take off your clothes and wash and all of you, mind, no skimping, and your hair. I'll find you something else to wear, those clothes aren't worth keeping.'

She left him there without another word, shivering upstairs until she was completely sure he had finished and she went back downstairs to find him clad in her father's old coat from behind the door, sitting by the fire. His now clean black hair shone in the firelight and his thin face was smooth. She gave him the clothes and made herself busy at the sink in the pantry until she was sure he was dressed and to her surprise he fitted her father's clothes. She had not realized he was older than she had supposed, perhaps even older than she was, and her father had never been fat.

'What are you called?'

'Harry – Darling.'

She stared.

'You've worked the markets before?'

'No,' but he looked hard into the fire as though he could deflect further questions, so realizing this she asked him nothing more.

Her father came back singing, she heard him from where she was trying to sleep upstairs and from experience knew what would happen next and when the singing stopped and the first chair clattered to the floor she hurried downstairs. There was only the firelight to see by but Harry looked up, an alarmed expression on his shadowed face, and she beckoned and somehow amidst her father's stumbling form and ragged steps Harry made his way across the room to the stairs and followed her up.

It was cold and it was only then that she hesitated, one bed in each room. She could condemn Harry to the other room but her father might find his drunken way to bed eventually and she could not take the chance that he might be violent. She had learned to stay away from him at such times and she rather regretted that they had done so well that day. Soon he would be cursing God for having taken his wife, crying and swearing.

There was a hot bottle in her bed, whereas downstairs the fire had almost died. Harry stood there, hesitating.

'You can get in,' she said.

He looked at her and she saw the colour leave his face and something more, she wasn't quite sure what, but she thought it might be fear which was surprising but made her feel more confident.

'You needn't worry,' she said, 'I won't touch you,' and he turned away and he pulled off his clothes and slid into bed. She got in at the other side. He fell into sleep as she imagined a child might, she had never slept with anyone before but as his breathing evened she somehow remembered the warmth of her mother's body even when they were inches apart and her mother's voice lifted with the morning or the days which she could not usually think of when her father and mother were one. It was somehow reminiscent of her early childhood, all those times that she could not remember.

Five

The following day her father was so ill that he could not get up to go to the market which was at Heath Houses just beyond the city. She and Harry loaded up the handcart and she was glad he was there. Usually when her father drank so much they could not go to the market at all because she could not pull the cart by herself.

She let Harry choose what they would take but she could see after that that it did not matter what it was, he could sell anything. He talked to the people who came to the stall, he held their attention either by being funny, by flirting with the older women or just by talking about the item they apparently wanted to buy but hadn't known they did until they got there.

Before the afternoon was over they had sold almost everything and Shona looked at the takings and leaving him there she went off into the town and bought a single bed from the second-hand shop where she bought everything she needed which was not much. She also purchased another pillow and sheets and blankets and food for the evening.

'I could go on sleeping downstairs,' Harry said.

'It isn't decent. This is the best we can do so we'll have to manage.'

He hesitated for a few seconds and then he looked straight at her and he said clearly, 'You needn't worry, I won't ever get in your road, not after what you've done for me.'

They collected her purchases, secured them on the cart, and when they got in the door, her father got up from the fire and demanded the day's takings and she said, 'I spent it. I bought Harry a bed.'

He could hardly object to that, at least he could have but even he must have seen the previous day that the boy had talent. He said nothing except, 'You aren't putting that in my room.'

They ate and it was a good meal, she had made sure she

bought potatoes and vegetables and a huge pork pie, she did not want her father going drinking again though to be fair he rarely did this two days running.

She and Harry had lifted the bed inside and up the stairs and she made it up. Harry made no comment about the bed which she pushed to the far side of the room away from hers.

The next day was another market. By then she rather expected that they would do well and had already stopped taking note of it but because her father was there Harry was inclined to give her the takings so that she made sure her father was not aware of all that they had. She had always done this to a certain extent, even her father did not think they could live completely without money but she secreted a good part of it and when he complained that day and said he thought there was not enough she turned on him.

'This stuff is old. You've had some of it for years, cluttering the place up, and now that we are selling it you seem to think the money is magicked from nowhere when we have to charge rock bottom for it to get anything at all and even if there is some it's to buy new stock, not to go down your throat!'

A year or two before this he would have taken the money from her almost without any kind of fight because she was so small, so slight, but they both knew that this was no longer the case.

'I buy the stock.'

'The only decent stuff you've bought lately was the scarves, and we wouldn't have sold those if it hadn't been for Harry. I think we should sell different things and I want to get rid of as much as possible so that we can use that room.'

'We've always stored everything there.'

'It can go in your bedroom since you've space in there.'

'And who's going to carry it up the stairs – and don't say him, you've known him three days. He could bugger off and leave us at any time, probably with the takings.'

'He hasn't done it yet,' she said and she went back to serving, pleased that for the first time ever she had bettered her father.

She determined to buy new things. All her life she had dreamed of owning a shop, thinking of herself in some high-class jeweller's, wearing a black velvet gown, selling diamonds and silver to people who could afford it and to have a carpet upon the floor so thick and soft that feet would barely be heard upon it. Not a big shop, something small and discreet, and for there to be good living space above so that in the evenings she could retire there to read and think and plan.

She could even see her name above the door in black and silver, Shona Hardy, Jeweller, and for her to employ a watch-maker so that she could do repairs and she would learn about precious stones, the countries where they came from, the way that gold and silver were mined, and she would be able to tell people that silver had been mined not far away in Weardale. Perhaps her shop would even be in Silver Street, how appropriate was that?

In the meanwhile she and Harry talked over the fire when her father had gone to bed and he asked her whether she knew people who made things.

'What sort of things?'

'Quilts maybe, jumpers, you know.'

'I don't buy stuff like that, it's specialist, I buy cheap from the big warehouses, at least my dad does, and besides, a lot of people make their own.'

'You have to give them something they can't make or can't get otherwise. Rugs? Curtains? Crockery?'

Many women made their own clippie mats so she didn't think rugs was a good solution. There was somebody in the town who made high-class rugs with wonderful patterns but they were too exclusive to sell on a market stall. Women made their own curtains too but she was happy to sell lengths of material and different kinds of net because living so closely in the terraced streets people liked their privacy and almost every house boasted net curtains so they settled on the idea of curtains.

Net curtains were frequently washed because they held the dirt but some did not last very long so she bought different qualities, patterns and lengths and when the wind was not too severe or the rain she tried to find different ways of displaying them.

Harry was good at this, he was good at so many things she could not imagine what it was like without him even after just a few weeks, he made a kind of rail which fitted around the stall but under the sheets which kept out the worst of the weather and there she could display the nets. Those made from silk lace were far too expensive for her customers but cotton was much cheaper and they came in so many varieties and styles with so many patterns and shapes that the women flocked to her stall.

It did not seem to matter that with the nets the drop on them was shorter or longer than the window, some people liked them short so that the window ledges could be cleaned often and the curtains were kept out of the dust which gathered. Some people preferred long because they looked fuller. The women would hem their own according to their tastes.

She had realized also that there were different ways to hang them. If you didn't have much money you could have just the bottom half of the window hung with net, there were lots of variations and the more she spent time discovering these and showing them on her stall the more the women of the city came to see what she was doing today that was new.

There were no rules, just like in any other kind of selling, she thought, there were also voile curtains which were very fine and delicate and almost transparent and some were made more interesting with decoration but others were so unadorned that the weave of the curtain was enough to satisfy some customers.

Some she displayed full length with a big scooped bit out of the middle in a loop so that people in the house could look outside. She was able to order them direct from Nottingham where most of them were made after Harry, who scoured the papers, saw an advertisement and suggested this to her.

She still knew nothing about him.

'Did you go to school?' His accent, she thought, gave him away as a poor child but then sometimes he changed his accent when they worked to suit his customers or just to be funny. Many poor children had never been to school.

He didn't answer.

'Where did you learn to read?'

'Don't know.'

He hid behind the newspaper. He read avidly when it was wet, when he was at home or any time at all when they were not too busy. He bought books, both stories and books on things like other countries and history, and he got them cheap from little shops in the various towns where the markets were. Harry could get anything cheaply.

She had discovered now that he said 'don't know' to any question he didn't care to answer and this included everything which had happened to him before he reached her house on that winter's night. So she still knew nothing about him but she had long since stopped worrying about whether he would steal, whether he would leave. They were making a lot more money because of him and she offered him wages at the end of the first month but he just shook his head.

'Don't need nothing.'

'You mean, "I don't need anything."' Shona had been schooled so far back that she barely remembered by her mother over such things as general grammar for she had the feeling her mother didn't care for the local dialect which Harry spoke most of the time, thick Durham.

'Or that either,' he said with a grin.

'You might.'

'When I do I'll let you know.'

She was therefore somewhat surprised the following week when he did just that, explaining that he needed some money but not what for, and he took a couple of hours off in the middle of the day and then came back without explanation.

When she arrived home that evening and went upstairs her bed had been transformed. It stood away from the window a little and the window had new nets which she had put up herself but the bed was now a bower, she thought that was the word for it, it had tall wooden posts at its corners and a square of wood at the top which all connected up and over the whole thing was draped trails of net tied back to the posts which could obviously be gathered along at night on the kind of rails which people used for the net curtains in their windows. It was the first womanly thing she had ever had and she stood dumb in the middle of the floor.

Harry was hiding downstairs. Not obviously but he was fussing over the table and the dinner such as he never did. Shona made her way slowly down the stairs and into the kitchen.

Her father had taken to sitting in the front room since she and Harry had moved the stocks of curtains upstairs into his room.

She was glad to be able to clear that room and they lived in what she regarded as a more civilized way and she would put on the fire – it was more work but she didn't mind because now she had help with everything and they would sit on the old settee. She had promised herself when they had more money she would buy new things for that room, curtains and chairs and a Turkey rug, but in the meanwhile her father slept away his evenings by the fire in there and was not going to the pub half as much as he used to.

'I thought the money was for something you wanted,' she said.

Harry was busily laying the table.

'Lasses need privacy, don't they? You don't have any,' he pointed out.

'One of these days,' she said, 'we'll have a better house, then we can have a room each.'

However when she suggested this to her father he would have none of it.

'I lived here with your mother and I'll die here. I'm not moving anywhere.'

She could see what he meant, she knew that the memories of her mother were all that was left for him and that somehow he kept them alive here but she could not think that her mother was ever happy in such a place.

'Hey, Harry, will you lend me five shillings?'

Shona did not attend particularly to this. It was Fred who had the stall across the market. He sold plants and usually did very well but spring had been late that year, there had been weeks of freezing weather since early December. Now it was the end of March.

Snowdrops and purple and white crocuses were only just showing along with green spikes of promise which meant that daffodils and tulips would be giving colour in the next few weeks but up to now every day had been a trial of ice and deep snow which turned to slush for a day or two until the weather hardened again. Fred had sold Christmas decorations with holly and mistletoe and other leaves and berries but many people had not been able to afford such gaieties and she knew Fred was struggling to pay his rent, two doors down from where they lived.

Harry came to her.

'Give me five bob for Fred, will you?' he said.

He had not asked for a penny since he had spent money on her bed so she should not have been reluctant. She hesitated.

'Howay man, Shona. He'll pay it back. We're going to have a spate of fine weather for Easter and people will be buying plants.'

She looked doubtfully at the grey skies and then handed over the money from the purse which she wore secured around her waist at the front. She heard Fred say gratefully, 'I'll have it back next week.'

'I'll tell you what, Fred,' Harry said, 'keep it for six weeks and pay me threepence extra at the end of that time.'

'That would be great,' Fred agreed, and off he went.

Harry was right about Easter. The skies cleared, the wind dropped, the sun shone, the daffodils bloomed and on Easter Saturday people came into Durham in their thousands. It was St Cuthbert's Day that week, there was a special service at the cathedral, children played marbles on the grass down by the river, couples picnicked on the banks below the castle and Fred sold out of plants.

He immediately offered Harry the money back but Harry said to him, 'Why don't you go out and buy twice as many plants while the weather holds with the money you have now, then you'll double your profits.'

'What if it rains?'

Harry laughed as though he was asking about rainfall in the Sahara.

'It isn't going to rain,' he said scornfully.

'It's always changeable. You can never tell.'

'If it rains before the middle of next week you can keep the five bob and the extra,' Harry said.

Fred went off, ecstatic. Shona went around from the back of the stall.

'What are you playing at?' she said gently. 'It's bound to pour down before then.'

He looked squarely at her for the first time and that was when she noticed how much he had changed now that he was being well fed and looked after. His pale skin was so clear, his dark eyes too, he was much taller than she was.

'Have you never taken a chance on anything?' he said.

'Trouble comes along all very nicely on its own,' Shona said grimly, 'and if Fred can't give you that money back I'll take it out of your wages.'

He smiled at that because he had no wages and Shona relaxed a little too. She was even half sorry when the sun continued to shine and Fred continued to sell the primroses and primulas in dark red and yellow and blue which brightened his market stall. She was so keen on the idea of getting one up on Harry, just so that she could tell him she had told him so and they would laugh.

'People like spring flowers best,' Fred told her, 'especially when it's been such a hard winter.'

This was true, she thought, she had longed for some sight of colour and had been grateful when the first snowdrops pushed their way through in the churchyards and the celandines showed their small spiky yellow faces amidst a sudden rush of green.

After that it rained on and off but Fred continued to sell more and more flowers as the time went on and the varieties increased because he could afford to buy them, much to the delight of the local people who wanted to stock their gardens with something different or new and on the day that the money was due he gave Harry sixpence instead of threepence.

Harry gave it back to Shona without a word but everybody knew what Harry had done and within that week Mari who was foreign and sold strange oils and coloured soap and candles and sweet-smelling essences for ladies who were lucky enough to own a bath or even care to add a little to their water as they washed morning or night came to ask Harry for help.

Shona sometimes bought some of the essence and put it into the water when she bathed ever so sketchily in the pantry which was the only place she could be sure that her father or

Harry would not walk in on her while she was busy. She loved the spicy exotic waft from the hot water as she took a flannel to her body.

Mari gave you wonderful little coloured bottles which she bought from the glass-makers in Sunderland and the bottle always seemed somehow to fit the person, a colour or a shape which was just right, blue bottles which held a silver light, red ones which glinted blood-coloured and green ones which had peppermint in them and yellow ones which smelled like crushed crocuses.

There had been a problem with supplies that week and she came and asked Harry if she could borrow a little money and he said the same thing he had said to Fred except that he left Shona on a quiet Wednesday and took the train to Sunderland to find out what the problem was and came back with the bottles Mari needed and some others which had been hand-painted, were just that day in, and she was delighted with these.

The little painted bottles sold straight away. He had also brought her painted jars and tiny vases into which corks had been fitted so that she would have other containers in which to sell her wares. The paintings were of red and blue butterflies or small wild flowers such as bluebells.

He even went over to help Mari bottle the special essences and he helped her to make the small translucent squares of soap and she experimented and began to use herbs from the garden and flowers as they came through the grass and by summer there were a dozen new essences which people recognized, lavender, rosemary, several different roses coloured dark crimson and light pink and yellow and white and mauve.

The new essences were recognized by the people who bought them and because they came from nearby they were so much cheaper to make than the exotic ones she had used before and had had to buy in specially from abroad and so she made a bigger profit and when she returned Harry's money she gave him extra and Harry gave it straight to Shona.

Shona did not give the profits to her father. She gave him some but every time he had full pockets he got rid of it in the pub, he was always buying rounds and she could hear, even at the house, the sound of singing from the pub at the end of the street, the Mill Race, and she knew that her father was buying for all and would come back with empty pockets. She could not bear that she and Harry worked so hard and her father got rid of the money so quickly so she began to deny him altogether. Harry didn't think it was a good idea.

'It's all he has.'

'He has me and he has you.'

'That's not the point.'

'Then what is the point, Mr Clever?' She glared at him.

They were standing at the back of the stall and it was raining and the rain was dripping down the edges of the sheet which covered the stall and all around the market there were deep puddles that day and nobody had come to buy anything.

'He has to do something,' Harry said. 'You have your life to go through but your father's life is over—'

'No, it isn't!' she fired back. 'If he would just – if he would just—' and then a sob caught in her throat and she couldn't say any more.

'Give him it, it's only money.'

Shona continued to put money under the floorboards in her room. Harry knew she did but she was not prepared when she came back in after the summer to find the floorboards lifted and the money gone. She started out of the house but he got hold of her for the first time ever and wouldn't let her go.

'He's taken that money to the pub. The whole bloody street will be singing.'

'There's worse things.'

'That money was for my shop,' she said, shaking free. 'I was going to wear nice dresses and sell nice things—'

'There'll be plenty more in time.'

'How do you know that?'

Harry didn't reply and she ran upstairs and slammed the bedroom door and went to bed without eating. Her father was gone most of the night and Harry did not come to bed. She heard a noise and when she turned over it was light beyond the curtains and she heard Harry talking softly to her father as he helped him up the stairs. Her father was not singing, he had got beyond it, he had got to the stage that he sometimes did when he was very drunk and it was then that her mother appeared to him and he thought she was there and would talk to her in a low voice.

Shona pulled a pillow over her head to shut it out. There were various sounds from next door, her father's boots and the squeaking of the bed as he lay down and Harry's soft tone, almost like a son, comforting, but when the sounds stopped Harry's footsteps went off downstairs and then she was sorry because it was not his fault, at least she didn't think so.

She tried to sleep and couldn't and eventually she turned over so many times that she gave it up and she flung on a shawl and went down the stairs in her nightgown, imagining he had gone to sleep on the sofa to find him sitting over a dead fire as though there was still something to be seen amidst the flames.

'I lost my mother.'

'Aye, but he lost his wife. You can't get it again no matter how close you might think you come.'

'You don't get your mother back either,' Shona objected and then subsided as Harry looked at her. 'Other men marry again, some of them very quickly,' she said.

'They're the lucky ones,' Harry said. 'Some people marry and marry again if they lose the second person and are happy again and again and they can let go but the rest of us – we hang on, we hang on like hell to everything that's gone.'

'Why don't you come to bed?'

'Can you stand me there?' When she didn't answer he said, 'I will make gold for you, Shona, if it's what you want.'

'All I want is a chance but I don't want anybody else getting it for me, I will do it myself,' and she went back upstairs.

After a long time, when she was almost asleep in the silence and dawn was about to break and the wretched birds were about to sing and the river was about to come alive and the streets would soon throng with those who got up early like the milkman and the delivery men, Harry made his way so very quietly upstairs and stripped off his clothes and got into his bed and lay there like a stone.

It was only when she could hear the evenness of his breathing which meant that he had given in to sleep that Shona closed her eyes and she thought for the first time ever she would not get up and go to the market.

For once it would get by without the sheets which covered her stall and the items laid out for sale as best she could arrange them, the sun glinting on the colours and the way she watched for the prospective buyers approaching, some of them strangers, some of them regulars, and she would remember the names of the people she knew and greet them and ask after their families and talk about what a beautiful morning it was. It was indeed a beautiful morning and as the sun crept between the curtains and began its assault upon the floor she closed her eyes and went to sleep and cared nothing for any of it.

Six

People continued to borrow from Harry until sometimes they did more business like that than they did with the curtains and Harry was very often so busy talking to other people that Shona would be left alone to sell. It was not only the business people who came to him but people from the town. Word had spread. Shona was much more careful with the money now and did not leave it in places where her father might find it and he was obliged to come to her and she would dole it out.

He protested that it was not right, that he worked as well, but the truth was that they did not need him now, he was more of a burden and if she gave him money he would go to the pubs around the market squares of whichever place they were in that day and make friends, the kind of people who liked having drinks bought for them.

Harry didn't care for this.

'He'd be better if he had summat to do,' and despite her brushing aside the idea he rented a stall next to them every day and would put on it to sell whatever her father desired. Shona treated this as an indulgence they could not afford.

'Will you stop being angry with him, he's done his best.'

'He couldn't give a penny loaf to a starving man without falling over, I don't know why he ever took to doing this.'

'I think it was what he wanted for his family.'

'I know nothing about his family.'

'Don't you have relatives?'

'You are somebody to talk,' Shona declared and it was true in a way, she felt uncomfortable thinking about such things.

That day, as though the very talking about it had caused the air to change, a man came to the stall when her father had gone to the pub for something to eat so he said and she was doubting, now that he had money in his pocket, whether he would return to take over the stall before the afternoon had ended. Harry, unable to leave anything alone, Shona thought, had got her father on selling rugs and carpets, stair runners and those that went up people's hallways.

'They're heavy to lift every day,' she had objected as Harry brought yet another big multicoloured rug down from her father's room.

'You were the one who wanted everything upstairs and besides, nobody's asking you to do it.'

'You'll end up selling them all yourself, you know what he's like.'

It was true, Harry was invariably left to do the stall because as soon as her father had enough money he would go off to one of his favourite drinking places and they would be lucky if he came back before teatime and would have to go searching for him in the various pubs in the area.

Also Harry had ordered rugs from wholesalers and was always off to the station to collect them. She thought this bad enough in itself since the station was on a long and winding hill at the top of the city. She should not therefore have been surprised, she thought, when Harry turned up one day with a new cart pulled by a very able-looking brown horse with three white socks. Harry got down and looked at the creature and rubbed its nose.

'This is Julius. I bought him from a man at the Three Tuns, he was retiring to somewhere warm and he's a good horse.'

'And where are we going to keep him?'

Harry looked at her as though she was mad.

'In a stable at the Three Tuns, where did you think we were going to put him, the back room?'

'That will cost money.'

'Aye but it'll be much cheaper for us in the long run,' Harry said and he was right. Every morning Harry went there to collect the horse and cart and every evening he went there to stable the horse and rub him down and feed him and talk to him and often she went with him and grew to like the animal's velvet nose.

So they ran the two stalls together and her father spent his days in sweet oblivion in the pubs of the area, playing darts and dominoes and paying for rounds.

So the day that the man came asking for him she said that she could not be sure which pub he was in, it could have been the Dun Cow in Old Elvet that day or the Victoria in Hallgarth Street, two of his favourite haunts.

'I haven't seen him in years,' the man said, 'I went to the church first to see whether they knew anything of him.'

'Which church?' Shona asked.

'St Margaret's, just up from Framwellgate Bridge. Your mother and father were regular people there at one time and your father being a vicar's son it seemed natural.'

If Shona had been drinking tea at that point she thought she would probably have choked.

'They were very respected, well-off people from the Tyne and so disappointed because they wanted him to become a vicar. He was handsome, he looked just like you except that his hair was darker, your mother was the red-haired one but he had incredible blue eyes and a ready tongue and he was charming and every girl in the area liked him and wanted to be seen with him. Your mother and I were about to become engaged and then she met him and she threw me over.'

'And my mother's family?'

'They were very upset because although he was talented and ambitious everything he touched seemed to go wrong after the marriage and by the time they had you there was nothing left. Your mother was often ill and he could not make life comfortable for her and I think they lost whatever happiness they had had. It was very sad. He went to pieces when she died, blamed himself. I tried to keep in contact but he shunned his friends and I moved away and lost all contact.'

'Are any of my family left?'

'No, they were both only children and your grandparents had very little to do with either of them after that.'

'They must have wished she had married you,' Shona said, looking at his neat clothing and rich appearance but he only shook his head and smiled and went away.

When Harry came back to the stall he could see that something was the matter and since there were no customers she told him and she could not help saying, 'All I wanted was a family.'

'Isn't it all that anybody wants? A good family of course, not a real one. People sitting around the fire and at the table, eating good food and making wonderful conversation. I never saw one like that. Did you?'

She shook her head. They were home early and her father was in bed soon afterwards and Harry said to her, 'Why don't we go out?'

She didn't know what to say. Her father had rather put her off but she knew instinctively that it wasn't what he meant.

'Dancing at the Assembly Rooms.'

'We're not old enough to get in.'

'Go and change your frock and I'll put on one of your dad's old suits.'

It was strange really, they could have been her mother and father, because he wore her father's only decent suit which was very dark and made him look older and which her father had not worn for years because he went nowhere but the pubs and she wore a dress which she thought she remembered her mother wearing and sometimes when things were very bad she would run upstairs and put her face into the depths of the cloth because she thought from somewhere her mother's perfume lingered.

It was a pretty dress, long and trailing like a handkerchief and slightly low cut but not indecently so and it showed off her white neck and shoulders and the gleam of her hair. She put on the only ornament she possessed which was a brooch her mother had left her, it was not diamonds but it sparkled like them and when she came downstairs he got up and looked at her in a way in which he had not looked at her before and he said, 'You look so beautiful, Shona,' in such a natural way that she could not help but laugh.

They went off to the dance and it did not matter that they did not know anything about it because the music was there and people were ready to help them learn and seeing they knew nothing a man led out Shona and a woman looked after Harry and taught them the steps and in very little time they were dancing together and the music was so in keeping with how she felt that Shona knew it would be one of the best evenings of her life.

They had champagne.

'Is it really champagne?' she asked, gazing down into the wide-lipped glass. 'I never danced before and I never drank champagne and I'm very happy.'

When it was late and the champagne was drunk and the bottle was empty he ordered more and Shona knew for the first time what it was like when you had money, you could order what you wanted, have life as you chose. The second bottle was even better than the first, cold and sparkling and with that special taste, not cheap and not sweet, and every bubble was bliss.

She could see suddenly why her father hid in little pubs with big fires where the ale was golden brown and the glasses clinked and conversation flowed and men stood around at their ease and dogs lounged and slept and snored. The world was always outside, cold and hard and taking things from you, but there among the champagne and the music and the way that Harry had learned already to place his hand so firmly upon her back she realized her father's loss.

She could not imagine what it was like when you never danced again, when you had no partner to say to you, 'Let's go there,' when nobody cared and you could not find the strength to go out and chance your hand again.

Women anyway could not do such things but her father might have and been accepted but he had not done it. In a way it was wonderful and in another way it was awful as if he had given up on life and opportunity and the possibility of happiness again. She understood for the first time and then she shuddered because she did not want to know that much, she did not want to comprehend what her father had suffered because she loved him and yet despised him for his weakness.

She pulled Harry close and as she did so he tightened his arms around her and she was then for the first time hidden from the horrors of her existence, of the idea that things would be taken away and she would be alone in that house in Paradise Lane. She had not known until then that that was her fear, that it was everybody's fear and that her father knew it first hand. If you believed as she believed that you had only one existence then how could you bear to have its very essence taken away from you and go on?

'You won't leave me?'

'I'll never leave you, Shona.'

She knew that her father and mother had said such things to one another and that it was not true and that you could not rely on it but she needed to hear it and she thought, from the way that he held her so near and yet so very carefully, that Harry Darling knew it too. She waited for him to kiss her because she knew that was what happened next but it didn't. He didn't hold her any closer or say that he loved her.

The following day she blamed the champagne, she was so embarrassed. Not that anybody had done anything. She and Harry had gone home and properly left one another space to undress and go to bed and nobody had said anything. They had not even touched on the way home as though the assembly rooms had been a dream and nothing more and the following morning they were too busy, even though it was Sunday, to talk.

Harry had gone to the stables to find that Julius was lame and he had spent most of the day there with the vet making sure that Julius had everything of the best and though they might have talked if she had gone there too her father was unwell, it was not the drink for once, his chest was bad. It was one of his body's failings, winter and summer he got colds which left him wheezing and hardly able to get out of bed, and she had ministered to him and then she had done the housework.

Other people went to church on Sundays but it was her only day to do things like washing and ironing and generally clearing and cleaning. She did her shopping all through the week from the other market stalls but she made food ahead every day so she did not have the chance to go and see how Julius was and was only relieved when Harry came back in time for something to eat in the early evening and reported that the vet had said Julius must rest for that week and he had made alternative arrangements so that they could get the goods to the market which they always attended on Mondays.

By the time they had eaten and she had seen her father comfortable they were both too tired to talk and Harry fell asleep with the newspaper in front of him so that it fell off the settee.

Seven

The young man across the way had been watching her for some time now. There was nothing especially new about that, young men frequently watched her, Shona had grown used to it. She did not count herself beautiful but her red hair stood out even on the dullest morning and she was seventeen now and many a man was looking for a wife. She worked too and that impressed them. She might have money, she was certainly capable and some of them knew also that she ran her father's house and had looked after him for years. The more unscrupulous would think nothing of moving into Paradise Lane and living off her and the more upstanding of them saw her as a good partner for the future.

This man walked over to her and there was something about the way he walked and she could not after that take her gaze from him because he walked from the hip and somehow as though each step was important.

Shona couldn't believe the effect he had on her. She noticed the slimness of his hips and how tall he was and how the sun shone so apparently brightly on his dark hair, giving it a sudden silver sheen. He had dark eyes and he smiled very slightly, not as though he expected anything just as if he was happy with the morning.

She had been happy too when she awoke. She worried about feeling happy first thing, she knew that something would be sure to spoil it. It was better to awaken from bad dreams with nothing left in you but relief and the shadows of the pictures in your head as they thankfully faded. Then she would get up to face the day with no regret but no expectation either. Today had been different and she was still suspicious so in spite or perhaps because of her initial and up to now unique reaction to this man she did not know she did not return the smile.

'Buying nets, are you?' she said.

He looked at the flimsy white curtains as they moved in the brisk breeze which had only just got up. Shona followed his gaze and watched for a few seconds as the wind worked its fingers through the various curtains as though examining them for quality and somehow as the wind lifted the white material it reminded her of a shroud and she shivered.

'My mother might but just now she's gone to look round the cathedral.'

She couldn't place his accent except to know that it was somewhere north of Durham. He looked at the other curtains too and they were also worth seeing, rich reds and deep blues and greens, and the material too for those people who would make their own for economy's sake and also because they were good at such things and there were lighter curtains and lighter colours, pale blue and cream for summer days.

Many of the better-off women in the place changed their curtains during different seasons, some had given up because often summers were cold and wet and it was more important to keep out the draughts but this summer was long and golden and all but the very poor had bought light delicate fabrics with which to adorn their windows and she had done very nicely out of it.

Harry had found a new Sunderland supplier and some of the new stuff had lovely patterns, bluebirds and spindly bare and black branches on a cream background and one in particular in cream with green ferns which she had sold a great many of since the weather had turned warmer.

'I'm James Rainbow. Will you tell me your name?'

'Shona Hardy.'

He reached out across the stall to shake her hand and she felt obliged to take his cool slender fingers and wish that her father and Harry would not return soon. Her father had gone off to some pub and she had sent Harry to find him almost an hour and a half since. She had been wondering where on earth they could have got to but now she didn't care.

Vexingly and with awful timing Harry came into view across the Market Place. He was alone which meant that he had taken her father home to bed, he would not have stopped looking for him.

He probably found him on the floor of one or another of the pubs nearby and had spent the rest of the time trying to persuade him home, bringing him round, holding him up, guiding him as best he could, back to Paradise Lane so that he could spend the afternoon sleeping it off.

Sometimes she rued the day that Harry had turned up and they had begun to make money. She tried to keep as much of it from her father as she could but Harry was wont to give him what he asked for so when he came back like this they would spend the afternoon speaking shortly to one another until the animosity died between them.

Partly because of this when James Rainbow asked her if she would go and have something to eat with him she agreed.

'Can you manage without me for half an hour?'

She did not give Harry the time to reply, just smiled in his general direction and left. It was a lot to ask him to manage two stalls by himself and usually she wouldn't have done it for more than five minutes and they would be busy all day but she hurried out at the far side of the stall and went off with James Rainbow, disappearing across the market square and into the steep winding road where Silver Street went down to the river.

She took him to the Silver Street cafe and there they had sandwiches, cakes and tea. He didn't look particularly prosperous but he was not poor either, all done up in his Sunday suit and shiny polished shoes. Somebody obviously looked after him, his mother, no doubt. Some mothers must be like that. Thinking of her own mother made one strong memory come forward, how her mother would read her fairy stories and in them there would be princes and princesses but since she had been alone for so long with her father and seen how he was and how mundane her life she had dismissed the whole idea of how you might care for one person.

She thought of dancing in Harry's arms but Harry was family, she had taken him in, they slept in the same room for heaven's sake. The idea of sleeping in the same room with this young man made her cheeks warm and brought her gaze to her plate.

'Is it too hot for you in here?' He sounded concerned.

She shook her head.

'You aren't from Newcastle?'

'Just below Alnwick. We live in a fishing village.'

'You're a fisherman?'

There was pride in his eyes.

'I have my own boat,' he said. 'Is that boy your brother?'

It was a good thing Harry wasn't there, she thought. He wouldn't like being called a boy.

'More or less,' she said and then she told him how she had found Harry in the snow.

'He must have been grateful.'

Grateful wasn't a word she would have applied to Harry, it was too passive somehow and Harry was never that. Her father came between herself and Harry, she had not realized and it was only now that she understood. Her father preferred Harry. She sat there shocked, no longer wanting the lemon-curd tart she had chosen because it was pretty.

Her father had always been disappointed that she was not a boy and she had tried to be in some ways to compensate for this disappointment yet she had looked after him like a good daughter, at least she thought so. She felt guilty for how she had treated him since the drinking had grown worse and yet she knew it was only because she wanted him to live and know if it was ever possible to be happy in spite of what had happened to them.

She did not go back to the stall that afternoon. She did not realize how the time had gone. They walked around the river-banks and talked and it was only when the shadows were long that they went back to the Market Place and it was empty.

Even then she lingered, she could not bear to let him go. She walked to the station with him, she saw him on to the train, his mother and brother would be long since gone, he said, but she thought it was just that he did not want to see them and before he got on the train he kissed her for the first time.

She watched the train out of the station and then she floated all the way back to Paradise Lane. It was only when she got home and saw that her father was upstairs in a drunken stupor and that Harry was just finishing putting the last of the rugs and curtains up there in the room with the unconscious man and there was nothing in the house to eat that she felt guilty. She had intended to shop and cook and had done neither.

'Shall I go and get fish and chips for us?' Harry offered, just as though nothing had happened and she agreed and he went off.

When he came back half an hour later she had lit the fire for the evening was chilly and they sat over it and ate the fish and chips from the paper and drank tea when the kettle finally boiled. She did not want to eat, she was happy to stare into the flames, but she felt she had to and when they were finished, when she had put most of hers back into the paper to hide it, she turned to him and said impulsively, 'Harry—'

'No, don't.'

She stared at his face in the light from the fire and the lamp on the table and against the shadows his whole countenance seemed darker to her than ever before.

'You don't know what I was going to say.'

'That you spent the rest of the day with him, that you like him, that you know you should have helped,' and he picked up the papers and threw the whole thing on to the fire where it spattered a little because of the burning food.

'But how—'

'Because that's what happens. In the end people always leave.'

She was about to say she would do nothing of the sort but he got up and took hot water from the boiler beside the fire and poured it into a jug and then he went off upstairs with the jug so that he could wash before going to bed. He didn't come back down again and Shona sat over the fire and thought of how James Rainbow's mouth had felt on her own.

Nothing had ever felt that good. Nothing in the whole world could alter it and best of all he had said that he would come back the following Friday, Friday being traditionally a fisherman's day off, and he would come to the market and they would meet up again and spend as much time together as they could. In the morning she would have to tell Harry that.

James wrote to her that week, assuring her of his affection. Shona had never received a love letter before, read it over and over again in private, carried it around with her until the

Thursday of that week when somehow it escaped from her pocket. Discovering the loss she got down and searched under the stall only to come up against Harry's long legs and brief enquiry, 'I think I've found what you're looking for.'

She got up and he held out the precious envelope and immediately she panicked, thinking he might have read it but too embarrassed to ask. She had resealed it carefully and it was still like that. She didn't look at him, she said a careless, 'Thanks, Harry,' and stowed it in a different pocket as she turned away.

Early that Friday morning she told Harry that she was taking the day off.

'I cannot run both stalls and do everything,' he said. 'Why didn't you tell me before?'

'You can have a day off when you want one.'

'I have nothing to do with them,' he said.

'Don't go to the market, then, have your own day off,' she said and she went upstairs and put on the prettiest dress she owned and walked up to the station so far ahead of time that when the train arrived she was almost jumping up and down from frustration.

She thought at first that James had not come, that he had changed his mind. She scanned the platform, her heart plummeted and then lifted and she could not believe he was hers, so tall and handsome. She stood dumbfounded and then he saw her and waved and she ran to him, shrieked his name and was enveloped into his arms. He kissed her, briefly since they were on the station platform, and then he let her go only to place an arm around her while they walked down the steep road back into town.

She felt as though her feet did not touch the pavement. It was such a good day. They went rowing on the river, they ate at a little backstreet cafe in the gloom where no one would know her and in the evening he took her dancing to the very place where she had been with Harry. There was such a difference. Time floated past until it was late, until it was the last train home and he must go.

'Shall I come again next week?' he said.

'Oh, every week. Every day if you can.' She kissed him as he got on the train and then she thought how far it was to go home in the darkness. She saw a figure in the shadows. Harry emerged. She was aware of irritation.

'What did you do, follow me?'

'I just assumed he'd take the late train. You can't walk back though the town by yourself, not at this hour.'

She was then aware of what she had said.

'Oh, Harry, you are good.'

'Aren't I?' he said drily.

She stopped there, guilt overwhelming her.

'I shouldn't leave you to do everything, least of all put my drunken father to bed.'

'He was singing,' Harry said lightly.

'Anything interesting?'

'"Auld Lang Syne",' and they both began to laugh.

In the end she didn't have to be brave and say it, Harry said it for her.

'You're going with him, then?'

She had thought there would be time, she had imagined how she would say it and how it would be received by her father, she had not anticipated that Harry would ease the way for her and she had tried not to think how he would manage after she was gone. He would manage somehow, he always did, and after all there was nothing between them, not like she had with James, but still she did not want to see the expression in Harry's eyes.

'He's coming to the house next weekend to ask.'

Harry looked surprised.

'To ask what?'

'To ask my father if he can marry me, of course.'

Harry looked amazed.

'Marry you?'

'Why yes of course. What else did you think?'

'Well that – well that . . .' Harry ran out of words. And then found them. 'You can't marry him, you hardly know him and—'

'And what?' she said, the anger rising.

'You know nothing about him, about his family or his circumstances or – he could be anybody.'

'He's the man I want to marry,' she said and strode away from him down the hill towards the town.

That was what she remembered, when it was late and Harry lay across the room from her, sleeping. She listened to his even breathing and she looked across at him and understood what he represented. He was the only security that she had ever known. That was a shock. He made her feel safe, both here and when they worked, like nobody could get past him, but it was James Rainbow she wanted to be close to.

She dreaded the Sunday. She didn't know whether it would be best to try to tell her father before James arrived or whether to let the surprise take care of itself. Either way, she thought, it didn't really matter.

In the end she thought she should prepare him and since he was at his best after breakfast before he had been to the pub at lunchtime the morning would be the best time.

'We're going to have a visitor on Sunday,' she said.

Her father looked amazed and she was not surprised as such a thing had never happened before. He said nothing. She glanced at Harry. He would normally have gone to sort out the horse and cart and begin loading it by now. She was glad he hadn't.

'He's a – a fisherman.'

Still her father stared.

'From Northumberland. He's been – he visits Durham some-times and—'

'He's a what?' her father said.

She could feel her face warming.

'A fisherman.'

'He's a long way from home, isn't he? Why is he coming to see us?'

'Well, because . . . because I asked him, I've been seeing him and—'

'Oh,' her father said, suddenly comprehending, 'it's like that, is it? Well, he won't be coming here, he won't be seeing me and he certainly won't be seeing you. You're far too young to consider such things and you have a good home which you won't be leaving for a very good long time yet, miss, so you'd better make sure he doesn't waste his time,' and he walked out.

Harry followed without a word so that she realized he had been there only for her. Nobody spoke all that day and she was glad to get on with the work, it was such an easy escape from confrontation. She tried to pretend that nothing had happened, she kept her mind off how upset she felt. When the day was over and it happened far too quickly she wondered whether her father would refer to it again but he did not. He had been in the pub since midday or before it, she doubted whether he remembered anything. He ate his tea and then he went out again and she said to Harry, 'In some ways it was better when we had less money, he couldn't drink as much.'

'Nothing else was better though,' Harry said and she had to admit that this was true.

For once the weekend came too quickly and she went to the station to meet James off the train and she tried to prepare him for her father's hostility.

'He doesn't want you to leave him,' James guessed.

She took him home and it was the first time she was ashamed of where she lived and she wished more than ever that her father had allowed them to move. She had asked James to Sunday dinner. Harry had said he would look after it while she was away and she could not help but see that James looked ashamed to see a man taking meat from the oven and prodding vegetables with a fork. Had he not noticed the wonderful smell?

She introduced the two young men and Harry left his cooking and came over and they murmured greetings as young men did and she went across and took out the tin from the oven and the tin was bubbling nicely with fat and she poured into it the Yorkshire pudding mix.

When Harry came back over for a second she whispered, 'Where is he?'

'At the pub.'

Her father came back just as they sat down to eat. She introduced them, her father sat down without a word and ate and when he had finished he got up and climbed the stairs and soon after this she could hear him snoring. At the table they were so quiet that all she was aware of in the room was the clatter of cutlery. There was a crumble and custard to follow but as they cleared the plates James said, 'Why don't we have it later? We could go for a walk.'

She looked at his open face with gratitude and then thanked him softly and minutes later they escaped the house. Too many people were around on Sunday afternoons so she could say nothing but when they reached the shadows of Elvet Bridge she burst into tears.

'I wanted it to be so different,' she managed.

James didn't say anything to that. When she stopped crying he said, 'Do you really want to come with me?'

'Of course I do.'

'Then you will have to leave him and that is how it should be.'

She couldn't speak for the tears she hadn't cried, so many of them left she thought she would burst with frustration and misery. She just shook her head.

'Let's go back and talk to him. He'll be out of bed by now, won't he?'

She didn't want to but they went and James was right, her father was sitting over the fire, drinking tea, and he looked narrowly at them.

'Do you remember me, Mr Hardy?' James asked.

Her father merely looked at the fire and then spat so that it sizzled. She had never been so ashamed.

'I want to marry Shona. I have my own boat and—'

'I don't care if you have a fleet.' Her father smiled gently in acknowledgement of his own wit. 'She has enough to do here. She has a home and a job and a family who cares about her. What do you want her to do, sit around mending bloody nets?'

James nodded and smiled.

'It isn't quite like that,' he said, 'except for the visitors and photographers.'

'Aye well,' her father said. 'She's going nowhere.'

'I want to marry him,' Shona said. 'I care about him.'

Her father looked scathingly at her.

'You're only a bairn,' he said.

'I'm old enough.'

'You're not marrying him, not a man like him. I'd give you to a well-set-up man, not a fisherman, not somebody I don't know and couldn't trust. How could I let you go with him? Your mother would turn in her grave.'

She almost said to him where would this gentleman come from but then she remembered her company and she thought she had disappointed her father that all she could catch was a fisherman. The phrase was horribly appropriate somehow.

'Mr Hardy,' James tried one last time, 'I make a good living. I can afford a wife. I will rent us a nice cottage and—'

'A cottage?'

Her father threw the words across the room as though they were living in a castle. James loved her too much, she knew then, to point out the hovel they were living in and she was very aware of Harry in the shadows beside the fire.

'I love Shona very much and I think she cares for me. Please let us be married.'

James, she felt, had never begged anything of any man before and his words came out haltingly.

'Get out of my house!' Her father screamed and shouted, said the words so many times that she looked pleadingly at James until he went to the door and quietly left.

There was a long silence in the kitchen which her father endured for the short while before his mind pictured a pint glass brown with ale and a foaming head and he could stand his thirst no more and then he took his jacket from the back of the door and went out.

For a while nobody spoke and then Harry said, 'Don't do it, Shona. For once he's right, you know it. You have no experience of the world—'

'And you have so much and so does he?' She said the words scornfully.

Harry looked down.

'He just loves you and—'

'If he loved me he'd let me go.'

Harry groaned.

'That is such rubbish. If only people loved like that, nobly, but they don't, they grub around in the darkness, desperate for just a sight, for just a second to spend with their children. His wife died. How will he stand your leaving?'

'What about me, don't I deserve my own life?'

Harry looked into the fire which had grown low because nobody had seen to it and down at his hands in the gloom. At that moment there was a banging on the door and when she opened it the man she loved filled the space and he was smiling at her and she found herself smiling back and her whole body warming and leaning toward him.

'Come with me now, Shona,' he said.

She glanced at Harry. He wasn't looking at her. She took a step back and then another and in the end she went to him and she remembered the market and the rain and how it collected where the top sheet was not secure, little pools of rain, and he would come along and make sure that nobody got wet, he would spill the water so that it ran into the road, into the gutters, he would feed the horse and talk to him and set him up for the day and he would load the cart, and in the night his breathing brought her peace and she would miss it.

She said, 'Goodbye, Harry,' and she thought he said, 'Goodbye, Shona,' but she was never sure afterwards that he did, maybe he didn't look up and she had imagined the smile on his face and the way that his eyes urged her to try to take her attempt at happiness, when she remembered him in her dreams it was so and her honest self would report to her that he had faltered then but she did not let herself believe it or she would not have been able to walk out of the door and she had to do that, it was the only way.

Beyond the door there was James and the future and all the wonderful days to come, a house, a home and children and being close and warm to his back in bed and eating with him in the evenings and making up the fire and thinking up delicious meals for when he came home. The coming home would always be the best, she knew.

Eight

The old man – Harry thought of him as the old man though in truth he was not as old as many men but the drinking had bulged and reddened his nose, puffed his body, ruined his complexion. His hair was so thin it was wispy and his bald pate sat dully beneath – he came back so drunk that he remembered nothing the night that Shona left and Harry was waiting up for him and as he fell in the door – and at least he did that, he hadn't had to be searched for – went to him and it was then, strangely, that he made the first kind remark Harry thought he had ever made. He looked at Harry through the numbness of drink and he said, 'You're a good lad, Harry.'

It was not the first time that Harry had wished the stairs were not so steep, not so dark, it took him a long time to get the old man up and in by the narrow doorway and on to the bed. He lit the lamp. It was just like a thousand other times and yet it was not. The room did not alter except that every week when Shona cleaned it everything was moved slightly because she dusted the furniture and polished it and she mopped the floor until the whole place smelled of pine disinfectant which was not unpleasant.

The floor which was linoleumed was always shiny even under the bed, the rugs were taken downstairs and beaten on the washing line in the yard and the sheets on the beds were changed very often. The house was damp in winter and stuffy in summer, it had been badly built and vermin crawled out of the walls and dropped from the ceiling and she fought the weekly battle with the house and its surroundings to make it as clean and comfortable as she could until the bugs retreated under her care and died.

He should have insisted on moving long ago he thought and then smiled at himself. Her father would not leave this place and she would not leave him and now she had, for the only reason she would ever have left. She had gone and that was what made the difference up here, she was not down in the kitchen, boiling the kettle and making a sandwich for supper.

It was his favourite time, when the old man snored above and he would undress him as he was doing now and put him into bed and go back down and they would sit over the fire and talk about the day, the people they knew, the markets, the towns, the difficulties of the selling. He supposed it didn't matter very much but he loved it.

He pulled up the covers now around her father and then he walked slowly back down into the kitchen and tried to accustom himself to the idea that she was not there. He didn't sit over the fire, he banked it down and left it and went to bed. It was no better upstairs because her clothes had gone from the little wardrobe where she kept them and from the chest of drawers which were not properly closed. He left them like they were and spent most of the night aware of her empty bed and trying to recall what it was like when she was here.

In the morning, hagged from lack of sleep he went down and opened up the fire and put the kettle over it and when it boiled he made tea and drank two steaming cupfuls before going to see to the horse. When he came back the old man was downstairs. He didn't even look up. He was unshaven, half dressed.

'Where is she?' he asked steadily.

'She left.'

Tam turned his head quicker than he had done in months, his face full of disbelief.

'Gone out? Shopping now?'

Harry didn't answer that. He laid the table and got the loaf and butter and jam and he made tea but the old man went on sitting over the fire. In the end Harry left him there and went to the market. He had not been set up long when the fruit and veg man, Nobby, came over to talk to him. Harry was so busy that he hadn't time to talk about the bigger business that Nobby wanted to set up or the money he would need to borrow so that in the end Nobby said, 'Our Bev could come over and see to that if you could spare me a few minutes.'

Bev was Nobby's elder daughter and a good market woman

and honest but he didn't think she could manage both stalls on a busy Monday morning. He conveyed this with a look and Nobby said, 'I'll see if Ma will lend us Sally too,' and he went off and came back almost immediately with the two girls. They were pretty Durham lasses, fresh-faced as though they lived in the country but good at selling, good with money and as big an asset to Nobby as though they had been boys, and more, he thought, because they smiled at the customers and chatted and that brightened the day of many a poor housewife and Nobby was known for his reasonable prices and kept many a poor family going in fruit and veg which was not fresh enough to sell and get full price for.

The local children didn't need to steal from him, he kept the bruised apples underneath, they knew and he distributed them freely. He made a good enough living because his produce was fresh, it came by train early in the mornings and by cart from the station and the local folk knew that he prided himself on it.

He offered to take Harry to the pub, it being not far off midday, but pubs only reminded Harry that later he would be required to do the usual round of searching for Tam in them so he suggested the Silver Street cafe.

Nobby obviously considered tea shops as places for old women which made Harry smile though not so that Nobby could see. It was true, Harry considered when he got there, he and Nobby were not dressed for tea shops and he thought it was a mistake because sometimes he and Shona would come there and have cake and sit by the window and watch women struggling up Silver Street with shopping bags, children running about on the cobbles and the sun, which at the bottom of the street would cast its twinkling stars across the river at the bridge.

He deliberately sat as far away from the window as he could as to make the difference. The waitresses knew him in there and one came over, greeting him effusively. Nobby was obviously not used to tea and sandwiches at that hour but since they got their fruit and veg from him he didn't mind too much, Harry could see. He wanted to borrow some money and set up a shop for his girls.

'They might wed but then again – and even so I want

summat better than the market for them partly because I don't
want to be setting up the stall in all weathers when I'm old.
A nice cosy shop, that's what I want for them.'

'Did you go to the banks?'

'Aye, of course I did.' Nobby leaned over the table towards
Harry. 'But I don't own me own house. I've no—' He paused
over the word. 'No assets. I told one of them my lasses are
enough asset for any man. Will you lend it to me, Harry?'

The truth was that he had by now been lending out money
and getting it back at slight interest for quite some time and
in fact he would have to go to the bank himself and withdraw
some to lend. He left nothing in the house. The old man's
bank account too was healthy. Harry only gave him so much
to let him booze away.

He agreed to help and even then Nobby, halfway through
his second sandwich, having said he wasn't hungry in the first
place, asked if Harry would go and look at the shop premises
which he had liked. They finished the tea and sandwiches and
left, Harry tipping the waitresses as always.

There were a number of empty shops in the town but the
one which Nobby favoured was not the right place, Harry
could tell. It was in North Road and it was big. They looked
around it, came outside and Nobby said, 'You think it's wrong?'

Harry hesitated.

'Howay man, I want to know.'

'It's too big, you don't need that back room or the space
above. You don't need a back door, your stuff comes in most
days through the front in the early morning when it isn't cluttering up the street and you can use the pavement, a wide
pavement, put a lot of stuff outside. Don't you really think
that what you need is two small shops, like that place across
the road?' Harry indicated the vacant premises and then they
went to see another in Gilesgate near the top so that nobody
would have to carry all that heavy stuff too far.

'Mrs Nobby liked this one.'

Harry said nothing more but later that day, Harry having
spent no time at all selling in the market, they managed to get
to look round the other two properties and when Nobby
questioned whether his girls would like it Harry deputed two

other stallholders to take care of things and took the girls to the shops and suggested one for each of them with their names above the door and as he had thought they wanted their own businesses and were delighted.

'In the meanwhile,' he said, 'you can keep the market stall on and in time find somebody to run it and you and Lily will be able to do whatever else you want and the money will roll in.'

Nobby was very pleased with this arrangement, Harry sorted out the banking and that week they went to see Mr Hedley the solicitor and negotiated the buying of the shops. They also sorted out how to get the produce to where they wanted it and it was teatime before Harry had chance to pack up the stalls, load up the horse and cart, take everything home and then search the pubs for Tam. He found him unconscious in the Victoria in Hallgarth Street, the landlord apologetic but unforgiving.

'It's not good for the place, you know.'

Harry was out of patience by then and didn't answer. He got Tam on to his feet and eventually home and that was when the realization that Shona had really gone hit hard. There was no fire, there was no food.

'Where is she?' her father said again. Nobody had tidied up, nobody had cleaned.

Harry opened up the fire, went for fish and chips. He ate his, Tam only looked at the plate.

'That lad won't look after her, she'll be back.'

'They're getting married.'

Tam looked as though he had never heard the word before.

'I'll believe it when I see it.'

'You won't see it. He comes from the top end of Northumberland.'

Tam considered his by now cold meal once more.

'She has to come back. I'm her father, she cannot just leave me, it isn't right and she wouldn't do it. I've done everything for her.'

'Well, she has done,' Harry said. 'Have you finished?'

Tam got up and looked for his cap and jacket.

'You're not going back to the pub.'

It was the first time he had said such a thing, he would not have done it when Shona was there.

'I'm too tired to come for you again.'

'You don't have to come for me.'

'You're not going.'

Tam considered him. Harry was inches bigger than him, a lot stronger and younger.

'I want a drink.'

'There's some beer.'

Tam looked surprised. He had no idea it was kept in the house. He sat down by the fire. It was a horrible evening, which was to Harry's advantage. It had gone dark and the wind cut through the room and the rain battered against the window. He watched Tam downing beer but he had judged it right. The old man's body was exhausted and before long Harry was helping him up the stairs and into bed and he fell asleep instantly and began to snore.

Harry washed up and tidied up. He didn't want to spend a second night lying awake, wishing Shona was sleeping nearby, but he didn't have to go upstairs. He sat by the fire but he was too tired to stay awake, thinking about Shona. He was glad of that. He could barely manage the stairs again. It was all he could do to reach his bed.

Nine

There had been a time when the rain was always outside, where Harry could go to bed at night and listen to it drumming beyond the thick velvet curtains which bettered the draughts through the old window at Dragon's Field.

Rain was always better than anything else, always easier because he could hear or imagined he could hear the children playing in the summer sunshine when the evenings were long. It made it feel as though he would prefer that it was always winter because he was not allowed outside to play with them and the loneliness cut through the sunshine and made him sad.

That wasn't quite true because in the summer he could run on the grass with his grandfather's dogs, he was allowed to go anywhere that was not outside the gates. Other people came and went and he did not question it because it was not that the house was a prison, he could have left any time at all, any time he chose, as he got bigger.

It was just that the only person who mattered in his life was his grandfather and he would have done almost anything to keep the worry from the old man's face.

As Harry grew older his grandfather taught him mathematics and different languages and a lot of things about how the world turned and worked and gave him the run of the library that he might enjoy the books by the fire. Sometimes people came to the house, never women, just men, and his grandfather would be closeted with them in the library sometimes for most of the night and it seemed to him in time that the servants left and the housekeeping grew shoddy and his grandfather shook his head and said that times were not what they had been and that Harry was all he had in the world, the only thing that mattered.

Being the only thing that mattered sat heavily upon his shoulders. He could have gone away to school, at least he thought he might have, but his grandfather looked so down when he suggested it that there was no way that Harry could really have gone, though he longed for friends of his own age, somebody else to talk to.

When he got up on the third day of his grandfather not being well and not coming downstairs he went upstairs and made his way into the shadowed room and found his grandfather still in bed.

Nobody had been to open the curtains and he pushed them back with difficulty because they were so heavy, rich blue velvet, and as the light came in there was something about it which he could not like. It was a cold winter light from outside and it was weak, as though it would not last beyond the morning, and that was often true before Christmas, it was as though the sun was making its last effort before giving up for the long bitter winter.

It was enough light to show him that his grandfather was still asleep, not moving, but then as Harry approached the bed and his grandfather still did not move he could see that it was not because his grandfather was lying on his one good ear – he was deaf in the other – it was that his grandfather had died.

He did not move when touched and he was cold, he must have died in the night. Harry had seen animals die before but never a person but it was no different from when the old Labrador died, everything gone, everything over and finished, and Harry did not mistake it, his intuition did not deceive him for a single second, though he wished it would. He knew that he would not talk to his grandfather again, that nobody would.

He did something he had never done before, he walked slowly downstairs and went through into the kitchen and there Mrs Morrison was busy about the breakfast as usual. She looked at him in surprise.

'I think my grandfather has died, Mrs Morrison,' Harry said.

'Really? I thought he was none too good when he went to bed,' she observed and then she looked sympathetically at him and said, 'He was very old, you know. I'll send Vera for the doctor.'

Harry was inclined to hang about the kitchen but she looked askance at him twice so he went out into the hall and there he waited the very long time before the doctor came.

It was the longest day of his life, the undertaker came after him and Harry was shut out from the bedroom and then from the library. No fires were lit that day and the only time anybody said anything to him was when the undertaker came out into the hall to complain how cold it was. Harry barely noticed these things any more.

Gradually the fires had become fewer and fewer until there was only one in the library where his grandfather would fall asleep over the fire and presumably one in the kitchen so that Mrs Morrison could make the meals though those also were not what they had been.

Harry went into the kitchen to enquire about the undertaker's request to find Mrs Morrison putting on her coat.

'Where are you going?' he asked.

'I'm going home. I haven't been paid for weeks and I don't suppose I will be now,' and to his astonishment she walked out of the back door and went.

He could discover no one else left. There had long since been no horse in the stables, the old dogs had died. There was no one in the house at all as he walked around and each room echoed and he noticed then as for the first time that the rooms had emptied of furniture and of paintings, most of them were empty. There was only his bedroom and his grandfather's and the library where there was any furniture. He didn't like to go and interrupt the two men to give them bad news so he went on sitting in the hall until they came out.

The undertaker went off without a word but the doctor paused there, saying to Harry, 'Do you have any family?'

Harry got down off the chair and for a moment he was inclined to say that he had not but the doctor did not look the kind of man who would take in a boy and he had heard the servants talk of orphanages and such like in connection with him, they had not liked him at all, he concluded now so he said with false enthusiasm, 'Oh yes of course.'

The doctor still hesitated as though he did not quite believe Harry.

'You do understand that there is nothing left? That the parish will have to pay for Mr St Clair's funeral. All this is owed to other people and owned by others too. Men have bad habits, you remember not to pick up any of them.'

'Bad habits?'

'Gambling,' the doctor said and he walked out.

Harry had not realized that things like cards and dominoes which he had spent many hours over in his grandfather's library were bad things. They had played for pennies and his grandfather said it was good for his maths and he was very good at such things. Also chess and chequers. Those memories were precious to him. It would not have done him any good to have said anything positive about it anyway since the doctor had already gone and nothing remained but the echo of the slamming front doors.

It did occur to him that he should wait for the funeral, it was respectful to do such things, but he did not want to stay here with his grandfather's body and the night closing in. However he could hardly leave, having nowhere to go and no money, so he went back to the kitchen where the fire had grown very low and found plenty of coal to put on it and he sat over it trying to decide what to do next. He did not sleep the whole night through. Such a thing had never occurred before but then his grandfather had not died before.

The following day nobody came. It snowed and that was the only difference. Harry sat and watched it. The coal ran out and he did not know where the rest of it was and it was so awful outside that it was several hours before he felt brave enough to venture out there and by then it was almost dark and he was more afraid of being outside than of his grandfather's body in the room upstairs.

He had cried over the dogs that had died and now he did the same for his grandfather and for himself but not for long. It was strange how difficult crying was when nobody was there to notice. It seemed such a waste of time and energy which he was sure he could put to better use.

Two days later the men arrived and they took his grandfather away and one of them came into the kitchen and he said, 'You can't stay here, lad,' and he waited until Harry got up and went with him. They closed the doors and locked the house.

The way that the funeral was conducted made him want to

cry even more, sitting while some vicar he didn't know – and why would he, they had never gone to church, his grandfather was given to drinking brandy and calling the Lord names – rushed through the ceremony as though the place was on fire.

The coffin was so bare, not like he had thought it would be, nothing but thin wood, and they placed his grandfather in a far corner of the cemetery where Harry was sure the ground was very wet. He did not want to think about what would happen to the coffin, or indeed what would inevitably happen to his grandfather's body.

He did not notice when the vicar had gone. Nobody else had come to the funeral, and it was very strange, he had not thought that you went to such things alone and there was nobody left when the vicar had gone except the men who were throwing soil over the grave.

He had a horrible feeling that he might be taken into an orphanage, he had read of children suffering such things, he imagined horrid scrawny men gathering him up into smelly moist embraces so he left just in case somebody was lurking around though afterwards he wondered with a smile why on earth he should have imagined anyone cared even that much because it soon became obvious that nobody did. He had nowhere to go, nobody to go to, and once again the light had gone from the day.

He wanted to go back to the house but he had seen the men lock the gates and although he could have found his way around the back and into the house he didn't want to do that. He could not imagine being there without his grandfather, even his grandfather dead had been better than nothing, but what on earth was he to do now? He walked around and it got colder and colder and although he was not hungry and thought he might never be again he could feel the emptiness of his insides and think how little he had eaten since his grandfather had died. He had a vague notion that his parents could be somewhere but did you want to find people who had not wanted you? He didn't think so. He wished he had asked Mrs Morrison where she lived but he thought of her putting on her coat and knew that she would not want him near.

He wished they had even given him time to find a coat because the night was clear with a million stars so bright and they were only that bright when there was going to be a hard frost. The frost twinkled on the tops of the houses and the branches of the trees and eventually he found himself drawn to what looked like the best place to be. It was a pub, the lights were blazing, the warmth of fires was evident through the windows and he found himself getting nearer and nearer until the door opened and he was inside. A big man blocked his way in further.

'What do you want?' he said.

'Nothing.'

'Get out, then.'

Harry went, aided by a shove which landed him on the pavement. The pavement was cold and wet and he didn't see how he was going to get up from there but he had to so he pulled himself very slowly into a sitting position and then on to his feet but he didn't go any further, he didn't know where to go. He began to look around him for no particular reason.

There was a woman outside, she was in the shadows, she saw him there but didn't acknowledge him. She was wearing less than she might have been for the weather, no coat and her dress didn't come up to her shoulders even, it was low cut and Harry didn't like to look at the top of her breasts, it seemed so rude, and her dress was way above her ankles.

He didn't recall having seen a woman's ankles before and he looked away but she didn't move either back or forward as though she was a fixture in that place but even though it was quite obvious he was there she didn't say anything so he didn't go to her, there didn't seem much point, she was nearly as bad off as he was, otherwise why was she there on such a horrible night? She must have nowhere to go either. He sat and in the end after a long time she came to him. He wasn't looking up but he heard the clop of her shoes, her heels he thought.

'You all right, sweetheart?'

Harry nodded.

'Fine,' he said.

'Don't look it.'

Harry could hear her accent, not like his at all, he spoke like his grandfather, she spoke like the servants and so he made his the same.

'Bad day,' he said.

'Aye,' she said, 'me an' all. I'm going to give it up and go home. There's no takers. You want to come?'

Somehow Harry discerned that all that mattered now was money.

'I have nowt,' he said, and the memory of the servants talking among themselves somehow came to him, he had not known he was listening to them.

She laughed.

'How old are you?'

'Nine.'

'Well, you've got nowt nobody's gonna want, eh?' she said.

He got up and went with her, he had nothing else to do, but he was suspicious, he was suspicious of everybody now. They walked for quite a long way or was it just that he was tired and had eaten nothing? Eventually they came to the river and to the delectable smell of food and she stopped and she said, 'If you wait here I'll get summat.'

'You don't have to do that.' He had remembered his manners.

She smiled and she went into the pub and Harry, thinking about the last pub, waited outside even though the cold seemed almost unbearable. It was not a long wait surprisingly and then she came out and she had two pies, one in each hand, and she gave him one of them and he hesitated.

'Take it,' she said.

Harry bit into it and it tasted like heaven, the meat and the gravy and the pastry so light and so tasty, and he wished it was a dozen meat pies but he was grateful and she ate hers and then they began to walk again and eventually they stopped and then they went up a long narrow staircase which had no carpet and at the top of it was a tiny room with no fire lit. He followed her inside, worried but so desperate that he didn't care and there she got down and lit the fire and the lamp and he could see that she had furniture, a bed and a table and two chairs. She took a bottle from a shelf and got two glasses and these she filled with some dark liquid and she offered him one.

Harry took it. He hesitated. The liquid smelled so strongly that it made him want to move back but he was too polite to do that, he didn't want to offend the only person who had been kind to him in so long that he could not think who had done that before her so he drank a little experimentally and it made him choke, it was fiery and caught at the back of his throat, and then it went down and down into his body and it was warm almost as warm as a summer's day at home with butterflies and lots of flowers in pink and purple.

He felt it go all the way down to his guts and it was lovely. He took another sip and it was even better and by the third sip he had decided that he liked it. She gave him some more and since she was having some more he thought that must be the way to do it so he took it and drank it but very slowly like she did and it tasted lovely, even better than the first had.

She told him he could get into bed and so he did. He took off his jacket and then his shoes and he still had the glass in his hands. He finished the fiery liquid and then put the glass down and she laughed and she said, 'You can take off more clothes if it makes you feel comfortable. Don't worry, I'm not funny.'

He didn't know what not funny meant but he took off his trousers and even his thick socks though the bedclothes were cold to his feet but they warmed up because of the drink and the whole of his body warmed up and he could feel the heat of her body even though she wasn't that close and she said something like, 'Are you all right, my darling?' and then she drew nearer just a little way until he acknowledged that he was fine and then she went to sleep. He lay there listening to her even breathing and thinking how badly the day had started out and because of her it had ended better. He did worry slightly that she was odd and he knew somehow instinctively what odd was but she didn't move, she didn't even turn over, she just lay there like someone purely exhausted and slept on and her breathing was so deep and so thankful that she was given another day, another chance. Harry had thought that morning that he was well out of chances but it seemed that he was not quite.

He was inside, he had had something to eat and drink, he

wasn't sure the drink was something a boy of his age was meant to have but it was very nice and it helped him to forget about his grandfather and the grave and the awful vicar and the men who put him out and the man at the pub who wouldn't let him in. He felt as though in some way he had triumphed over them but it wasn't his own doing, it was this woman's.

What did she want? Nobody did anything for nothing, he had learned that now, but he didn't know what she wanted and although it made him feel uncomfortable as though he owed what he could not pay he didn't understand and since she was asleep and seemed to stay that way however long he listened and however long he waited for something worse to happen it seemed that in some daft way he had won the day at last and he was glad that he didn't have to offer up anything else before he was allowed to get away with another night of breathing and sleeping and then waking. He hadn't counted on it.

Somehow he had thought he would not live beyond his grandfather. Why was that? His grandfather was so old. He thought it was just that his grandfather had been the only person that he had loved. Could you live without love? Perhaps you could or perhaps you went on like an eggshell when the inside had gone, when the egg was cracked and heated in the pan and some person who was insensitive had eaten it; you did not know or care or could do nothing about the fact that the very heart of you had died and you went on, thin and without substance of any kind, without your insides, without anything left that mattered. You had to go on, what else could you do? You could not kill yourself, you didn't know how, and there was a traitorous part of you which wanted to live, which cried and screamed and pulled at you to be there.

He liked her breathing, in and out, in and out, and the sweet smell of the liquid they had drunk on her breath. He drew nearer so that he could breathe it in. Even then she didn't move, unaware of him, how odd. He couldn't have slept like that with a stranger but then the more he watched her breathing the more he wanted to close his eyes because of the warmth and the lovely smell of her and the way that day had been too much, so very hard.

He didn't want to think about it any more and he suddenly realized that he didn't have to. Why should he stay awake and worry? There was nobody to worry about any more. That was awful but at least it was a kind of relief and so as he listened to her breathing his own breath took on the rhythm of it and he went to sleep and he was so glad.

The following morning the fire was out, he had a headache and as he sat up he saw that she was writing a list of some kind.

'Can you read?'

He was about to say of course and then didn't, he just nodded.

'This is the shopping list. I want you to go to McGregor's down the road and see what you can get of this.'

She gave him the list, Harry read it and then he got out of bed and put on the clothes he had taken off the night before and then he waited.

'What?' she said.

'I need some money.'

She laughed.

'Do you have an account there?'

She laughed even more at that.

'See what you can take, let's see how clever you are.'

Harry stood. She meant stealing. He knew what that was.

'There's nowt to eat and I made no money last night, those pies were the last of it and there'll be no money today.' She nodded at the window where the curtains didn't quite close. Sleet battered the glass. 'Go on, then,' she said.

Harry wanted to refuse, he wanted to say the things which his grandfather had said, that it was wrong to steal, and he thought that such ideas depended on your circumstances. He was hungry again already, as though the pie had reminded him of food and urged him forward.

He left the room, he went down the stairs. There were other people in other rooms, he could hear the noises, they talked and moved around and somebody shouted. He clattered down the stairs and out into the weather and he wished again for perhaps the thousandth time that he had thought to bring a coat, some clothes and he wondered whether he should go back but for now he had to go to the shop and steal. It was a very strange and frightening idea.

The shop was full of people. Harry was amazed. Wasn't it early for such things? Perhaps it wasn't. It was the kind of shop where people bought all sorts of groceries. There were bags of potatoes but he thought they were a difficult thing to conceal about your person so he wouldn't take those and anyway they weren't on the list.

It was cakes and pies and he could see those, they sat in one of those long wooden displays over on the side. Nobody seemed to notice him even though he was the only child in the shop. He would have thought he would stand out. He was quite tall for his age too but he didn't look particularly unkempt because he wore a suit and for all his day outside and his night in a strange bed and the lack of washing facilities he still thought he was quite neat.

He managed to get a big pie in either jacket pocket while he was standing around with everybody turned towards the front waiting their turn. He was the last in line so nobody behind would see him. It was the easiest thing in the world, he discovered. He jammed cakes into his trouser pockets and on the way out a good many other things into a bag he found near the entrance.

How very odd that nobody saw him. Perhaps people only saw what they wanted to. Perhaps he wouldn't look so respectable for very long. If he had been dirty and ragged he would have been noticed, probably put out of the shop, but like this he jammed into the bag anything within reach so that he could do it without particular movement. When the bag was full he casually walked out of the shop with a feeling he had never had before, very heady and surely very bad.

He walked slowly back and up the stairs and into the room and then he very proudly gave her the pies, the cakes and the bag, and she stared into the bag and said, 'How did you manage all this?'

She laughed and then she said, 'What's this?' and she pulled out a large onion. 'What the hell am I supposed to do with it?' and they both laughed and then she made tea because she had lit the fire by then and they had a kind of sweet bread for breakfast, something Harry had not experienced before, and it tasted very good with the tea. He said this and she said, 'That's why it's called teacake, dafty.'

That day Harry decided he would go back to the house and retrieve some of his belongings. He was afraid but his outing to the shop had made him brave. She didn't try to stop him when he said he was going out or ask where he was going but he did feel he had to say, 'Can I come back?'

She nodded absently and he let himself out. It was quite a long way to the house and he had been right, the gates were locked, but there were plenty of ways around the park which contained the house. It seemed odd that having rarely been out of the place he was now not allowed into it but he got through the fence where it was broken down the side and because it was such a dark, wet and awful day nobody saw him.

It was strange going into the house and he went into the room which had been his grandfather's and then wished he hadn't, it was so awful remembering what had happened. The house hadn't been totally cleared and he went into his room and discovered his clothes. He went up to the attic and got down a suitcase and put everything he possessed into it and then he took another and he put everything that he thought might be valuable into that though there was not much, just some books.

He took everything back to her, left her with the suitcases and then he went all the way to the house again because he thought it might be his last chance. Today was Sunday and after that he would not go again. This time he found things in the cupboards downstairs, dried food, quite a lot of it, things like flour which was heavy but he took everything he could. He only wished there were some things he could have given her which would be just for her so he scoured the rooms and then the attic and in the attic he came across a trunk full of clothes, women's clothes, expensive ones, and so he filled another bag with those before leaving.

They were very heavy indeed but the sleet was blinding and few people were on the streets. He was very glad when he got back and she heard him and came down the stairs and said, 'You've never lugged all this stuff here?' and took one from him and hauled it up the stairs.

She didn't ask him where he had got it but when she opened the suitcase full of clothes her eyes lit. He didn't remember having ever made anybody's eyes light and it was a wonderful feeling.

'You pinched these for me?'

He didn't like to tell her that he hadn't but he didn't want to tell her where he had been and got them from so he didn't say anything and she didn't notice. She crooned over the satins and silks and velvets and over a pair of black shoes with shiny silver patterns.

That night the weather cleared and she left him there. He thought she might wear one of the dresses but when he said as much she said they could sell them when times were hard and Harry who had thought times were about as hard as they could get was quite surprised.

He was asleep when she came back and her footsteps sounded heavy upon the stairs and when she came in she had another person with her, a man. Harry would have pretended that he was asleep but nobody gave him the chance. She lit the lamp and when he sat up she indicated that he must leave. He didn't understand at first, he had assumed that he could stay, but she nodded her head at the door and when he didn't move she said, 'I need the room,' and that was all. The man didn't even turn around, didn't look at him, and Harry concluded that he was drunk. Perhaps they were both drunk because she had not spoken so roughly to him before. He was so taken aback that he went and heard the door slam behind him and a key turn in the lock and that was all.

He sat on the stairs, thinking that they might let him back in again, but they didn't. He considered going outside but it had begun to snow heavily when he ventured down the stairs so he sat there, getting colder and colder as the dark night wore its way through. His only hope was that she would let him back in again in the morning but the door did not budge and after he had tried knocking and then banging hard on it when the daylight finally arrived nothing happened.

He tried banging on other doors but again nobody heard

and after he had sat there until halfway through the day he went down the stairs and to the shop where he had stolen the groceries, only this time the man behind the counter glared at him and Harry realized that he had no coat and no shoes so he no longer looked respectable so he left.

It was market day. He hung around various stalls but the stallholders watched him carefully and if he hung around for too long they shouted at him. He walked back to the house but there was activity, men inside, and finally there was nowhere to go but back up the stairs and wait to be let in, like somebody's cat. The door did not open until another night had passed and then a man emerged, brushing past him, putting on his coat. When he had gone Harry banged on the door once again but nothing happened. She did not emerge. He tried calling but nobody answered.

It was the worst way that Harry had ever felt, nowhere to go, nobody to go with and worst of all no money. Before his grandfather had died Harry had never considered money, he was not even aware of it, and he supposed now that that was how rich people went on. Now it was the most important thing in the world, he was cold and alone and he was hungry.

His first instinct was to sit down and cry out of despair but he knew that wouldn't be any use so he tried going into the shops to ask for work but he knew how he looked and people shooed him straight outside. He asked at the market stalls too but it was the same response.

That night he had no strength left, he was beyond hunger, he felt sick and the only shelter he could manage was the doorway of a pub. He could feel the warm draught coming from inside and huddled closer to the door. Men went in and out and every time the door opened he caught a glimpse of the inside, the warm smell of cigarettes and beer, the sound of conversation which somehow was comforting and yet made him feel so left out, the odd burst of laugher. Nobody seemed to notice him or if they did they ignored him.

After a long time the door opened, somebody paused there and then said something to him and Harry sat up and the next thing a carriage and horses arrived and Harry was being bundled into it.

After that if there had ever been any normality in his life it ceased. There was a long carriage ride which seemed to go on for ever in the darkness with two men in the carriage as the night grew colder. They had rugs over them but did not offer him any and they did not stop in spite of the way that the cold came down. The carriage windows were blacked out so there was nothing to see so he thought it might have been snowing.

After a very long time it stopped and he was bundled out again and he wanted to protest but was too cold and too tired and all he knew was that it was up several steps and then inside. He was glad of the warmth but nothing else. Then there was a room and then a door opened and there was a cupboard. He was let go of then, not exactly pushed, just put down and the door closed and after that it was dark.

He had no concept of time, it could have been a week, a month, much longer, Sometimes they took him out for very short periods, to eat and to drink, water and dull food which was not distinguishable one meal from another. At first he banged and banged on the doors and when nobody came he shouted and shouted and when nobody came he cried.

When they let him out he thought at first that he would be released, afterwards he could not imagine why and because they did not let him go he did not eat and so they put him back inside and he was so enraged that he screamed and shouted and banged his body against the doors but although they shuddered they did not give and soon the only sound was his own voice and even that gave out eventually until there was no sound at all. Exhausted, hungry and thirsty he slept and he was glad of the sleep because it took away the hunger and thirst.

It was a long time before they let him out again and again he tried to get away and he begged not to be put back but the man who was there was silent and when Harry touched him he punched him round the head and Harry made sure that he got a drink of water and a slice of bread before they put him back again and then he remembered the room, how there was no light in it, the shutters were closed and only a candle burned and he could not see what kind of place it was.

They let him out the first time, except for food and drink

and when he had to relieve himself, when there was some kind of dinner party going on, the sort of food he had never seen before, all pink and red and green in a dining room to where he was led down a long corridor and then into a wide hall with a huge sweeping staircase.

The people sitting around the dinner table were dressed in fine clothes and huge log fires burned in the grates. The table was long such as the table his grandfather had had and at these times he was bathed and dressed and sat down with them and allowed to eat and drink whatever he wanted and the fine ladies stroked his hair and cuddled him and put him on their laps and sang nursery songs to him and he soon came to realize that he was the entertainment. They would encourage him to sing and although Harry never wanted to sing again his understanding was that he would not be able to stay there if he did not and he wanted the food so he sang, anything they liked that he could remember. They would stand him on the table and he would sing.

He understood that he was just a boy to them, they probably thought he was younger than he was because he looked young, he knew he did even though he was growing quite tall. A half-grown boy held some attraction for them. When the evening turned into night they would drink so much that they fell asleep at the table or the more sober ones went home and then he would be put back in the cupboard again.

As he got bigger he was required to let the ladies kiss him and he did not deceive himself that it was because they liked him, it was always for their own gratification, and he thought it strange that people like that wanted children near them in such a way. They wanted him to kiss them too and that made him feel quite sick because the only person who had ever kissed him was his grandfather and he would kiss him in the middle of his forehead every night before Harry went to bed.

In the cupboard Harry would remember these things and try not to think of his grandfather's huge fault which had been so costly but to remember only that his grandfather had loved him, that he was worth loving, that this was not loving, it was something so vile that sometimes he wanted to go back in the cupboard and sleep and forget it.

His only good times were when he slept because his dreams were his longings for his old life and for a better life and for this horror to end and for nobody ever to take his mouth like that again or to run their hands over the smoothness of his body and ask him to touch them in places he would so much rather not have done but his food and drink depended upon it.

He slept more and more and he grew taller and thinner so that the clothes they dressed him up in did not fit and there was never enough to eat and awful as the banquets were he longed for the food at them and came to despise himself for this weakness because the payment for the food was to be constantly a child and always entertaining, like a doll and not a person or a monkey which the organ grinders had or even a bear dancing in the street as in old times, how cruel it all was, his survival depended upon his performance and he grew very good at making jokes and singing and dancing and laughing and being kissed and kissing and being handled and fondled and told how beautiful he was.

He began to think that if he did not eat he would die and maybe it would be better but his appetite got the better of him always and everything they gave him to eat he took, he could not help himself and he hated the person that he became. The cupboard became smaller because he had become bigger and then there came a day when the cupboard opened and he was blindfolded and shivering at the sudden cold realized he was being taken outside and back into a carriage and it was a long time later when he was pushed out of the carriage and left and when he undid the blindfold he found that he was in a street he didn't recognize.

It was winter and it was snowing. He was down by a river and there were lots of horrible little houses, all leaning together as though they could not manage apart, as though they would all fall down, like in the nursery rhyme if they did not clutch at one another's stones just above the river where the snow fell leaden and almost colourless.

The whole world seemed colourless to him and the little houses went on and on, each one poorer than the rest he thought and it was almost night and nobody was about.

He had not the strength or the courage to bang on any door and he had not the energy because he had not eaten in what he thought was a very long time.

As the night came down he couldn't go any further. He went on sitting until he couldn't get up. It shouldn't have been a huge effort but he had been in the cupboard for so long that he couldn't manage it and as he became more and more tired he found that he was lying down.

The snow was soft and comforting such as the cupboard had never been, it had always been so hard and unforgiving, all that wood, and now the snow was thick on the pavement and it did not seem cold, it was like a bed beneath and a blanket above, and he closed his eyes and thought about his grandfather and then he fell asleep and it wasn't cold any more, his dreams were filled with big fires and good food and his grandfather reading to him.

He was therefore most upset and angry when he heard another voice, a girl's voice, intruding into all this. He tried to push it out but it wouldn't go away. Somebody prodded and poked and pushed at him and he was angry when he awoke because he was convinced he was at a banquet and all kinds of awful things were about to be required only when he opened his eyes the girl was looking down at him in the darkness with a lamp beside her.

She was about his age, he thought, though he was no longer sure how old he was and she was making him get up and he didn't want to, he just wanted to be left alone, but she wasn't happy, she didn't leave, she went on dragging him away from his soft snowy bed, away from the stars and the sweet darkness and oblivion.

Ten

Her new home was not what Shona had expected but then she was not certain what to expect when she reached Northumberland but she trusted James. It did not matter where they went or what they did just as long as he was there. She felt the sureness as she had felt nothing else and in a way she longed for the journey to go on and on because there was nobody but the two of them and the steady rhythm of the train which went through Chester le Street and Newcastle and on into Northumberland. The route was lovely along the coastline and she watched the blue of the sea and the little stone cottages on the cliff edges and lying on the shape of the coastline and she felt a freedom that she had not felt before.

The big surprise was when they got off the train at a tiny station, the only passengers to do so, and then into a horse and cart and after a very few minutes on a narrow winding road they came to the coast.

The village was surrounded by sand dunes which were covered in spiky grass and you came upon it suddenly because the landscape hid the buildings, some of the cottages were nestled low between two higher pieces of ground so that the winds both of the land and sea would go whistling over-head and leave the house below snug and warm away from the cold draughts which swept the sand into graceful whirls.

There was no harbour, she had expected something closed in, walls and piers and the North Sea beyond, but here was nothing but a beach and the boats, blue, white and black, or red with other colours like that, the darkest at the bottom, the colour in the middle and the lightest or white at the top, were pulled up at the edge of the sand where the tide could not reach.

She was astonished at how small the village was, especially after the city life she was used to. There was nothing here but the houses and a pub, no shops, no streets, no life at all, nothing to draw the eye from the little houses themselves built here and there as people had chosen, all of them facing the sea at either side of a narrow road which led away towards Alnwick and it was quiet, nothing but the sound of gulls and the tide making its way over black rocks.

When she mentioned the rocks to James that day he told her that these were only hazardous if you went near but all the fishermen who lived there had been born there, their fathers and grandfathers and those before them had been fishermen too, for time so far back that nobody had any idea where they had come from before it. They knew the coastline as well as they knew the lines on their own faces.

It was almost dark and very late when finally he stopped in front of one of the bigger houses and it seemed to her that he hesitated before he opened the door. The door opened straight into a big room which did as kitchen and sitting room she could see and there were a number of people sitting around the fire and when he took Shona inside one of them got to his feet, a tall lean young man. There was another of about the same age sitting beside him and a girl of about Shona's age and then an older woman.

Nobody spoke. Shona didn't know which was worse, the looks on their faces or the distinct smell of fish and some kind of oil which permeated the room.

'I've brought Shona. Shona, this is my brother Jack, my friend Collum – they share my boat – that's Joan, a neighbour, and then there's my mother.'

Still nobody spoke and Shona tried to say hello and that she was pleased to be there but in the silence that proved impossible. Jack finally said, 'Aw, you didn't.'

'I said I was going to.'

There was a low sob from the girl and then her face could not be seen in the firelight.

Jack regarded Shona like she was something he had hoped never to see.

'Did you not know my brother is betrothed and set to be married in a fortnight?'

'I'm not! I told you, I told all of you, that it was not what I wanted, that it would never happen but nobody listened to me,' James protested.

Further sobs but James turned to Shona and he said, 'I never agreed to it, it was something our parents decided years ago.'

The other young man, Collum, said to Shona, 'We don't marry folk from other places, especially not from somewhere as far as away as you were.'

Shona wanted to say that it was only Durham, that she was a north-easterner and had been all her life, she was no incomer and then she realized that to them she was and that anybody further than their village would be.

'You're not bringing her in here,' Jack threatened him. 'Apart from owt else look at her bloody hair. You'd end up with ginger whelps.'

'This is my house as much as yours.'

'I'm the eldest of us and if you choose differently you'll have to leave. You've chosen so get out.'

Shona tugged at his sleeve. She could see there was no possible way that they could remain. She was also angry that he should have brought her in here like this without telling her how unwelcome she was. He ignored her and shouted at Jack and the argument went back and forth, the girl's crying was now open, his mother shouted too and so did Collum so in the end she let go of his sleeve and left him there. She went outside and shut the door and when he did not follow her she began to walk back the way they had come even though she wasn't sure of the route, it was a very long way back to the station and it was dark.

She had not gone far, more than ten minutes, when there were running footsteps behind and he caught up with her and when she wouldn't stop he got hold of her. She was obliged to stop but turned around, saying, 'How could you let me walk into that? Why on earth didn't you tell me?'

'You wouldn't have come and I wanted you to,' he replied. 'It's the same thing you did to me. You knew your father didn't want you to go.'

'If I had realized the welcome I would get I would have stayed in Durham.'

'No, you wouldn't,' he said.

'You were getting married in a fortnight?'

'I never said I would, not once, it was just like nobody heard me, nobody wanted to listen, it was all arranged by other people and even though I kept on telling them I wasn't going to marry her, her mother and mine went out and bought her dress and planned the reception and talked to the vicar and it was as if I had no voice.'

'And I was to be that voice?'

'No. It's you I want, I only ever wanted you, first and last, I knew it would be. I did tell them but they wouldn't have it. Nobody ever marries out of the village, you see, nobody is good enough, nobody will do.'

'You must have known it wouldn't work out, why did you put us through it?'

'I just thought it might.'

'So what are we going to do now?'

'Go to my uncle's,' he said, though Shona could tell this was a spur of the moment idea, the only thing he could think of. He had expected that if he just went ahead and did as he chose that everything would be all right. She was astonished.

'Does he know about me?'

James shook his head but he took her by the hand and they walked a little further away from the village and then another house loomed, a small house, a cottage, and this time he did not bang on the door, he just opened it and it opened into a big room not like the other, this room took up the whole of the ground floor. There was a fire and she could see it clearly in the darkness and the outline of a man sitting over the fire and this place like the other also smelled of fish. It made her feel sick but she thought perhaps the circumstances were more to blame for that.

'Is that you, James?' he called and James confirmed it and closed the door behind him.

She waited, held back.

'Have you got someone with you?'

'Aye,' James said.

'Well, come in by the fire, then. Is it Joan?'

James moved her forward and the man said, 'Who are you?' and Shona realized for the second time that evening that she was a disappointment. She didn't think she had been that since she had understood that her father would have much preferred she should be a boy. Was she never to be a pleasant shock to anyone?

'I'm Shona Hardy, we're to be married.'

The older man looked at her even more curiously.

'Married?' He looked past her at James.

'I was never going to marry Joan.'

'But you are, in a couple of weeks. It's all arranged.' He nodded at Shona. 'Send her back where she came from.' And then he looked harder at Shona. 'She isn't in the family way, is she?'

He was talking about her as though she was not in the room and so insultingly that Shona didn't know what to say.

'You can't wed her even if she is. She's a foreigner, look at her, she didn't get that colour hair round here. She's not a Redesdale lass, is she? I once knew a star turn from there.'

Why didn't people know that you chose the one you wanted, that you knew it was right, that you couldn't help yourself, that it was the only thing you wanted even if it caused the stars to fall from the sky? Had they not felt the same? Had they let themselves be pushed into unions they did not want?

She thought again about the other girl crying her eyes out. Obviously she had wanted James, she had thought he was hers, gone along with it all and been pleased to, and his mother thought he should wed her. She thought of how little and sharp-voiced and faced his mother had been, of Jack's temper and Collum's words, and she was glad not to be there but where could they go now?

'We've nowhere to stay,' James said.

'Well, you can't stay here, your mother would never talk to me again.'

'So you go there and we'll have this place,' James said.

His uncle stared at him.

'You can't do that.'

'Aye, I can. If you want your place in my boat you leave us here. I'm entitled to a house.'

His uncle's eyes narrowed.

'You ungrateful bastard,' he said, 'I taught you everything you know. Jack would do this and your bloody father would've as well but you—'

'Leave us in peace,' James said. 'Get your things and go.'

'All of this is mine.'

'Aye well, I'll send it on to my mother's in the morning.'

The old man shuffled reluctantly out. James slammed the door after him. Shona stared.

'You can't do that, this is his home.'

James looked straight at her.

'I think you should stop telling me what to do. I'm not Harry, you know, licking your bloody backside all the time.'

In the silence which followed Shona thought of that horribly appropriate phrase about having burned all one's boats.

'Why don't you see if there's anything for us to eat,' he said more gently so she did.

There was a little room like a pantry off the kitchen, she picked up the oil lamp and took it in there, leaving James the firelight to see by. Various scurryings preceded her and when she got in there she was not surprised to find mouse droppings on the shelves and various covered plates and it occurred to her for the very first time that she had not thought to find a worse place than Paradise Lane. If only she could have told Harry he would have laughed and that was not a nice thought.

'Is there owt in there?' her intended asked when she had been examining things under cloths and dishes for some time and come across moulds and various disgusting smells.

'Not much.'

'I might have bloody known,' he said, coming into the pantry. 'There might be some cheese under there and there's half a loaf on the table. It'll have to do. And there's some beer.'

'I don't drink beer.'

'There's nothing else.'

The smell of the beer, once it was poured and they were sitting around the table, reminded her so much of her father that she could have cried and how stupid was that? She had wanted to get away from him and now she had. He sighed as she watched rather than eat the food on her plate and he put down his piece of bread and said, 'Look, Shona, I didn't know it was going to be as bad as this. I should have, I think, but I want you, nobody else. It maybe isn't what you expected but it's what there is. I know I'm not Harry—'

'I wish you would stop going on about him,' Shona said, raising her voice for the first time and being rather glad of that. 'I don't want Harry, I never did want him, I want you, I just didn't think it would be so – so awful.'

'It won't be awful. I'll sort things out. We'll be married in a month or so. I'll go and talk to the vicar and everything will be fine.'

'How can it be when your family won't have anything to do with us?'

'They'll get used to it,' he said. 'Are you finished?'

'I don't want it.'

She thought he got up to clear the plates and then he stopped.

'Howay then,' he said.

'Where are we going?'

'To bed. It's what people generally do at this time of night.'

Reluctantly Shona followed him up the stairs only to discover that the narrow upstairs of the house was low-roofed in a strange shape which tapered at one end.

'It's where they used to keep the sails,' he said.

He had carried the oil lamp upstairs. She had never before hesitated over sleeping in the same room with a man but this was different.

'There's only one bed,' she said, 'do you expect me to sleep with you?'

'It's the only thing I've wanted since we met.'

'But we aren't married yet.'

He gave a long deep sigh of exasperation.

'But we're going to be,' he said. 'Come here, then.'

Shona went. It was not anything like the way that she had envisaged it. Had she been able to find any humour in the situation she would have. She doubted if the room had ever been clean, there was no furniture save the bed and a chair, no water to wash in, no towels, and the bed itself was small, only just big enough for two people who really liked one another and her liking for this man was decreasing by the minute but it was not him, she knew, it was the stupid way he had handled this and then she was honest with herself and knew that she had been stupid too and Harry had been right. She should never have come here.

It was too late for that, he already had his hands on her breasts in a way that made her whole body shudder with need for him. By the time he lifted her on to the bed she didn't care about the cleanliness of the sheets or anything else. And then she understood. She had wanted this man for his long lean body and the sound of his voice, for his beautiful eyes and his way with words and for how he kissed which he was demonstrating now with great skill and she was needing more and more the feel of his hands and mouth on her body. It might not be love but she had not known there was a difference in such things until now and she could not have wanted him more, except that she did, she did not think she could ever have enough of him.

She awoke not knowing where she was but warm and happy and then she felt the smoothness of his body just as he awoke and got out of bed.

'Where are you going?'

'Fishing.'

'But it's still dark.'

'It won't be by the time I get things organized and anyway everything depends on the tides.'

'Do you need something to eat?'

'Is there anything?'

Both questions were equally stupid she thought and had to admit that she didn't know.

'Are there any shops?'

'In Alnwick.'

'That's miles away.'

'There is a carrier's cart and others I think and there's money in the dresser drawer. Try not to spend too much, sometimes in the bad weather we can't get out for weeks so I make nothing.'

'What do you do then?'

'Stay in bed,' he said and grinned.

When he had gone she was very aware of the smell of the

sheets and the grime against her bare feet so she got up. In daylight which soon arrived the place was even worse than it had looked the night before. She was used to poor housing but she had always kept her place in Paradise Lane as clean and well organized and comfortable as she could. She felt a pang for the place as she had not thought she ever would.

The first job was the fire. She cleaned it out, there were paper and sticks in a drawer beside the range and there was a huge pile of wood which by its variety had come off the beach. It was light, so well dried and this she fed on to the fire. There was water in the boiler next to the fire and when it had heated sufficiently she took the tin bath from where it hung on the outside of the house and put in it only enough water to wash and when she had washed and dried herself with the one cleanish towel she could find, which was in the pantry, she put on clean though old clothes, there was such a lot of work to do, there was no point in trying to look good.

Luckily it was a fine bright day. She scrubbed the sheets and blankets with good soap on the washboard she found at the back of a cupboard in the pantry, found clean ones in a drawer upstairs which had not been used in a long time. Some woman, maybe his aunt, had been a good housekeeper but she was long gone, Shona thought. There was nothing wrong with these so she changed the bed. After that she began her cleaning in that room. She put the rug by the bed outside to be washed whenever it was another fine day and then she scrubbed the whole of the upstairs floor. It took a long time.

She looked through the cupboards downstairs to see what she needed as far as food was concerned. The answer was everything. The flour had weevils in it and had to be thrown out. The butter, lard and cheese were rancid, the bread was mouldy and various creatures were living in the pantry, both on the shelves and the floor. She vowed to be rid of these but could not do everything at once. After that she found the carrier's cart as it passed her door and left the village with enough money to stock the pantry shelves.

Alnwick was a beautiful town. She was surprised, she was not quite sure why. She had thought she was coming to a place less civilized than the one she had left and was glad to discover that it was not so. She only wished they could have lived there, and not in a tiny village where she was not yet accepted.

The centre of the town was full of lovely stone buildings. There was a theatre and lots of shops and on the edge of the town the Duke of Northumberland had his residence. Tiny figures stood above the entrance to the castle. The gates were open and it was tempting to go inside but she could not of course. Instead she found a good butcher, a fine grocer and a good many clothes shops.

She looked in the windows of the clothes shops before going on to buy necessities for her kitchen in others. She had never had a pretty dress in her life, most of what she wore now had been her mother's. She had money in the bank and was thankful for Harry's sensible ideas. He had encouraged her, made it possible for the money to be hers so that she could take it when she needed to. It was a considerable sum. She and James had not discussed money but she thought if she did need anything and no doubt they would if he could not work, if the weather was bad for weeks on end, it would be useful and she must not waste it now.

Having bought nothing but food she went home, replenished the fire, cleaned the pots and pans, made a stew and the next thing she awoke to hear James coming home.

'A fine woman you are,' he scorned, smiling, 'asleep.' Then he stopped. 'What is that wonderful smell?'

'It's your dinner.'

'Oh my God. I find a beautiful lass and she really can cook.' He took the lid off the stew.

'Meat. It makes such a change from fish.'

'It was very cheap but it's been on there ages. It should be tender soon. There's plenty of hot water too.'

'For?'

'You don't want to sit down to dinner smelling of fish, in fact I would prefer it if you took off your clothes as you came in.'

'I've always wanted a woman to say that to me.' Good-humouredly he went back to the door, enquiring, 'Everything?'

'I'll get the bath.'

'Will you help me?'

'If you like,' she said.

He was impressed with everything she did and told her so and she basked in his praise and clamoured for his time and his body equally. She liked how he came back to her each evening. She liked how she gradually transformed the cottage into a home. She bought things for the home too.

'Where is the money coming from?' he asked.

'I have a little put by that I made working.'

'Have you now?'

She bought new rugs and material to make curtains, sewing over the fire when the days were wet and dull. She went to the salerooms in Alnwick and bought a wardrobe, a dressing table and matching bed and a new mattress. The old bed he chopped up and they used it for the fire.

She loved the days when he could not go fishing because the weather was too bad. They would stay in bed or go for walks, eat lovely meals and sometimes go into Alnwick where he insisted on buying her a new dress in green velvet, but though she hovered in front of the jeweller's he did not buy her a wedding ring.

'When are we going to see the vicar about getting married?'

'Next time I'm at home,' he promised.

A fortnight went by, three weeks and she began to worry because he had not mentioned the wedding but she should give him time. The following week she said on the Sunday, 'We should go to church. We could talk to the vicar about the wedding.'

'My family will be there.'

'We could go to evensong.'

'My mother goes to church twice every Sunday. I'm going nowhere near,' he said.

'But the vicar—'

'Will you stop going on about it?' he said loudly so she did.

When she had stopped having to clean so much, when the house was more or less to her satisfaction and she had got used to the comings and goings of the boat, things got easier to some extent and she had time to look about her, time to go down and watch for the boat and to notice the people in the village and it became obvious quickly that they would not accept her.

They ignored her, nobody ever spoke, she tried smiling, she tried saying good morning but they would look ahead or down at their feet. Nobody ever called and soon the uncle and Jack and Collum were no longer part of James's boat, he had other men with him. They did not speak either. If she went down to meet the boat they would talk among themselves so the only person she had anything to do with was James.

It was better if she went into Alnwick and she started doing that regularly because there the shopkeepers knew very few people and would talk to everybody and it was all the conversation she had. And she would buy the local paper and also she would go to the library and take out books and when she said for the second time one week that she had been into the town James looked at her and said, 'Have you got a fancy man there, then?'

He spoke in jest but she said before she could stop herself, 'I might do if you don't marry me soon.'

He didn't say anything and she said, 'Don't you want to marry me, then? Do you think we can go on like this?'

She was upset. She had walked through the village and heard the word 'whore' that morning and she was so ashamed because she had not intended this to happen and she felt her face burn and she dared not look up to find out who had uttered the word in a low voice, it could have been anyone.

'It isn't like that,' he said.

'Like what? We aren't respectable any more, nobody bothers with us.'

He looked at her then and his eyes were hard and he said, 'Yes, well, I never thought it would be like this, that I'd be cast out from my own family because of it.'

'So was I.'

'It's not the same thing. We have to live here.'

'I don't see why we should. The boat's yours.'

His eyes faltered.

'It is yours, isn't it?'

'Aye. Well, after a manner of speaking.'

'After what manner of speaking?'

James looked more uncomfortable than she had ever seen him.

'My dad left it to me with the idea that I would give Jack and my uncle a place in it because I was the best fisherman of us all. And I did. And—'

'And what?'

'That I would look after my mam first.'

It was an awful lot to think about.

'He was asking too much.'

'It didn't seem like that,' James said hotly, 'and he was dying. What was I supposed to do?'

'You were supposed to tell me all this, I think, before you dragged me up here.'

'I didn't have to drag you. You wanted to.'

'I thought we were getting married.'

'Yes, well, we aren't,' he said flatly.

'We aren't? What, you mean ever?'

'I was supposed to marry her, wasn't I?' and he went out and slammed the door after him.

She wasn't having that. She followed him. It was a filthy night, the waves were crashing up the beach, the wind and rain were blowing sideways.

'You what?' she shouted after him and he had not even the sense to leave, to go somewhere she couldn't get to him, he just stood there like a little lad, with his head down.

'I told her I would wed her and then I saw you. I wanted you like I've never wanted anything in my life, but her and me, we were bonded in the cradle and that's different.'

Shona didn't know what to say.

'You don't want to marry me?'

'Of course I want to. I cannot, don't you see?'

'No, I don't see. Tell me.'

'I just did.'

Shona knew what she wanted to say next but she could hardly get the words out. 'Are you going to marry her, then?'

'Of course I'm not.' He was shouting, against the wind and the rain but also against her. 'I love you. It never occurred to me that I could care about somebody like I do about you. I said I would marry her because I thought all a man wanted was to be in a lassie's knickers and I know that you think I wanted the same from you and it's true, I do want you so badly always, but coming home to you, it's just the best there ever was and that's the truth. I want nothing more than to come back to you every night for ever and ever and I know I'm stupid and I've got it all wrong but I couldn't help it. I saw you across that market square and I just knew that it was right.'

His voice was precariously wobbling and she felt stupid and she wanted to go to him and she wished she had never seen him and yet she remembered also the moment that she had seen him and loved him and it wasn't anything she would have wanted but she knew that she felt the same, that she wanted nothing for ever and for ever more but that he should come back up that beach to her and that it should never have any ending.

'You stupid bugger,' she said and the wind took her words away. She didn't even know whether he heard them.

'I love you, Shona,' he said and then she went to him and he turned to her and she wrapped him into her arms.

'We should leave here.'

'I can't ever leave for what I've done.'

'And we have to get married, I'm sorry that you've behaved like an idiot but we do. I don't want to be anybody's whore, not even yours, so either we get married or I go back to Durham, so make your mind up,' and she made herself go inside and leave him there.

It was such a gamble, she knew it. The fire had gone down and the room was cold and the wind and rain threw itself around the tiny house and she thought of how he had put his uncle out and had alienated his family for her and the horrible way that Jack looked at her when they met as though he was picturing her without any clothes and himself leeringly close. It was disgusting and made her shudder.

She waited and waited. Half a dozen times she almost went outside but didn't and she thought of the rain getting through his clothes. He probably didn't even notice because so very often he came back drenched and had been soaked through all the day because the rain had run down despite every effort to keep it out, down his face and down his ears and down his chin and down his wrists and arms and down his legs and his feet. She built up the fire twice before he came back and he was white-faced, shut the door as the wind banged and clattered outside and she thought she could hear even there the crashing of the waves.

'I don't know what to do. I've done everything I can. Please don't go.'

He came across to her heavy with the rain, his feet sopped on the floor, as he came to her he left great wet patches. He said he was sorry and Shona forgave him everything. She didn't want to and she knew she would be sorry a thousand times but she couldn't help that. She thought, you never get what you want, you never get the man you think exists, Prince Charming was only a story and they all have serious faults – her father, the other men she knew.

She brought Harry to mind and dismissed him. She had not seen his faults but they were there, they had to be, it was just that he had not shown them to her, had hidden them or perhaps had lost too much to come that close. It was true, she thought, you couldn't get close enough to Harry to see the real man, to identify the flaws. She knew her own, she was short-tempered, hot-tempered even, impatient.

She peeled the wet clothes off him and gathered him into her arms there before the fire on the thick kitchen rug and she didn't care about the things she wanted him to be or the dreams that she might have had from reading fairy tales, he was hers as nobody ever would be again, his body cold and wet from the rain and warm from desire for her. Nobody had ever wanted her with that desperation, that he should give up so much made her care for him all the more.

He had braved his family's wrath, put out his uncle from the house, endured his brother's taunts, she had no doubt, and as for his mother, she did not really want to think about that. She was woman enough to know that your sons were dearer to you than anything on earth. His mother would speak to neither of them, would not acknowledge his love for Shona.

It seemed ridiculous to her but she could see how in such small communities people clung to their habits, to ideas that had gone on for so long. His mother had expected him to marry a girl who had been his from the cradle and it was a good idea, they would have the same background, the same values, they knew the same people, their families were almost intertwined, and that would have been well and good if his mother had not expressed a desire to spend a day in Durham and see the magnificent Norman cathedral.

The cathedral no doubt had been responsible for a good many things but perhaps not often a love affair. Maybe it was not true. And that over the hundreds of years it had been there, it had seen all manner of people's desires, needs and wishes, and lovers had stood in front of it innumerable times and wished on its towers for happiness, for children, for a future.

His mother now must no doubt regret ever having seen the grey towers of Durham Cathedral. All you ever had, Shona thought, was our own destiny, not your sons' and not your daughters'. She thought of her father trying to keep her there, it was a puny defence against youth and it would not stand. You were not there to tell your children how to live their lives and even if you did they would not listen. You had your life, you made your decisions and that was all. Each man and each woman had his or her own destiny and no father or mother could keep them from it.

Eleven

Shona didn't sleep the night after James's funeral. The tiny house was freezing cold before morning, she just sat there in her coat until the day came late and then picked up her bag and walked through the little village to the station. It was three miles and by the time she got there she had changed the bag over from hand to hand so many times that both her arms ached. She took a train to Newcastle.

It was such a big station, Shona had forgotten. So busy, people going to and fro, women wearing fashionable clothes, those with suitcases going north to Edinburgh or south to London. She did envy them Edinburgh. She and James had once gone there to stay a night or two and it had been the most magical time, the dark stone which was the base of the city, the castle, Princes Street and the sweet lilt of Edinburgh voices.

Durham was home. She was scared, lost, her heart beat hard as the train left Newcastle station and in a way she wanted to hang back, run to Northumberland. She did not look at the tiny city when it came into view. She knew that on the left there was a view of the cathedral and the little town that spread around it which made people's breath run short.

She kept her head down and when the train halted she got off and then she walked down the winding hill and turned left into the town and she looked no further than she had to, across Framwellgate Bridge where the view of the cathedral and the castle was at its best because even though it was a cold day the sun and the wind cast shooting stars upon the water, the ducks paddled by the towpath as people fed them and everybody hurried by on the bridge because there was nothing to stop the wind.

The wind came off the River Wear much as it did off the sea, she thought, but it smelled different, it did not smell of salt and fish and somehow wide and open, it was a more closed smell of muddy banks and decaying orange-brown leaves and shallow places where the stones had been warm and deep pools where the fish hid.

The solicitor's office was beyond Framwellgate Bridge up the winding Silver Street, through the Market Place – she asked directions of a middle-aged woman and was surprised and shocked to hear the familiar tones of what had been her own accent – turning right then and going down on to Elvet Bridge and there the brass plaque on the wall read Hedley, Jameson and Hedley.

She opened the door. It was, to her surprise, a friendly place for a solicitor's office as far as she could judge, though not having needed a solicitor before she was unsure. A big fire burned in the reception area and beyond it sat two people, a man and a woman, both of middle age, behind desks. The woman was typing with an assurance which made Shona want to confide in the man instead and he was writing and she stood for a few moments until he looked up.

He smiled and said good morning. Shona handed him the letter and he frowned and then he said would she take a seat, he would not be long, and then he disappeared into the back part of the building and she waited. She didn't sit down, she was feeling too nervous.

Presently he returned.

'Mr Hedley has somebody in with him but if you would wait he will see you directly.'

Directly was promising, she thought, and so it was that a man came out of the office and was ushered out and then a tall well-dressed man in his early thirties came to her and wished her good afternoon and told her he was Aidan Hedley and would she care to come into the office.

She followed him. He sat her down and stood behind his desk for a moment or two as though he didn't quite know what to say.

'You have just received my letter?'

'No, I – I didn't find it before now.'

'It must have been a shock, then.'

She admitted that it was and he told her in soft tones how her father had died.

'I understand that you had not recently been in touch.'

Had Shona been happier she would have smiled at that, a bitter smile.

'We didn't speak, hadn't done for many years. I was nothing to him, you see.'

She asked Mr Hedley to read the will to her, if he would not mind, and he did so and she listened to the refined lilt of his polite northern voice and then lost everything but the sound.

She could hear the waves crashing to the shore and remembered once again that James was dead. She tried to think of the summer tide and how he had come home to her every night and how they had sat outside until it grew dark and when the tide was in they would watch the birds feeding and she had thought that she could not be happier than this and it was true, she was sure now that she would never be so happy again.

That summer had been their last, butterflies in the garden, willow herb purple in the lanes, grass warm beneath her bare feet and the slow ache of the evening when she and James would sit outside, mouth to mouth as though they had only just met.

Only just met. She heard it again in her mind. Now, knowing that you could not have that youthful love back again, she was amazed that it had existed and thrived in such a stony village disapproval but nothing could have stopped it and now that love was still here where there was so much pain because of it and she and James were beings apart.

Aidan Hedley read in his cool polite solicitor's voice and she watched him. He was such a young man yet he did an old man's job and did it so well you might think that he had an old man's body inside his expensive suit, hidden, neat, so that no woman would ever forget what he was saying and remember that he was a man and that his body was warm to the touch behind the cloth, young as James had been.

There was a legacy, it seemed. She looked across at him, blinking. She could not imagine that her father had had anything to leave her.

'He left me what?'

'A shop.'

Aidan Hedley looked as though he would have given a great deal to have avoided her eyes. Evidently it was not good news but then she had not expected anything good, she had come to believe that nothing good would ever happen to her again. The solicitor did not stutter but he had to stop himself and then he said a little offhandedly, 'It's a big place in the middle of the city, to one side of the Market Place.'

'What's it like, what does it sell?'

He hesitated again and she had to suppress a desire to hurry him up.

'It used to sell second-hand goods of all kinds,' he said and he sounded as though he wanted to give her some good news, as though he was personally affected by such a thing which she thought was an excellent quality for a solicitor to pretend.

'Like a glorified market stall, is that it?'

'Something like that,' he allowed. 'It wasn't a success.'

She wanted to scream and shout and say that nothing her father had ever done in his life was a success, nothing he ever put his money into worked, and we suffered, my mother died from lack of food and warmth and love and I went away. Nothing he did was ever any good. He had left her something that had failed. How very typical of him, she thought.

First of all though there was the trip to Paradise Lane to be completed. She wanted and did not want to go back there. It had been such a very long time and perhaps things had altered but when she reached the house where she had been born and brought up nothing had changed except that it was obvious to her then that her father had neglected himself, that he had not looked after the house, not cleaned or got someone else to clean. There were no signs that anybody had eaten there, no food in the cupboards, no dirty dishes in the sink but the bed had obviously been recently slept in and the sheets were filthy, she could hardly bear to look at them.

It was almost as if her father had resented her mother's death and her leaving so much that he had deliberately let it all go and yet she thought with honesty it was not really that, it was just that he did not concentrate, did not care to think about such things. Her father wanted to sell things, it had been the obsession in his life.

She did not quite know why, what had caused it, she only knew that she had seen her father with light in his eyes and joy on his lips when he was taking money from someone and giving them whatever they had exchanged it for. There were worse things, she knew, but it had been so important to him that it had cost him everything else.

The other thing was – and she did not want to acknowledge it – what had happened to Harry because there was no evidence of his having ever been there and he had but she felt guilty just thinking that she had left him with her father. What had she been thinking of? She knew. She had been young, she had wanted to get out. But Harry had been young too and he had not left, he had not gone, he had not thought about himself. Thinking of this made her hate him and despise herself and wish things differently. Harry had been there and she had not.

It was not a small shop, that was the first surprise for Shona, the building which housed it stretched the full length of one side of the Market Place. She stood on the cobbles and considered the building from across the street as though if she got any closer it would bite her. It was on three floors and above it must be storerooms.

The keys weighed heavily in Shona's coat pocket and she began to walk across the street towards the darkened windows and closed doors. It had been some time, she deduced, since the big front doors had been opened, the key would not turn in the lock, she thought it rusted. When she finally unlocked and opened it the sound echoed from the front to the back of the building.

Inside she could smell damp, mice. There were various scurryings. All was gloom, the cobwebs and dust were thick and the floor crunched under her feet. It was dark inside, the windows were far too small for the building, if you could have let light inside it would have made so much difference, especially considering that it was the very middle of the town and there were buildings all around.

She moved inside, the door slammed and once again the building echoed. It all made her aware of how long she had been gone.

In that time it seemed that her father's ambition had carried him beyond his capability and the money that he had not lavished on his child's basic needs had gone into this – what did you call it? A white elephant? It was like an indoor market but not a patch on the one across the street which had been built for that purpose and why would he want to compete, why buy something so like that there could be little custom for?

This looked and felt like a failed enterprise, like somebody had had a blurred vision, had not been able to afford or not had the money to endow it with decent goods. She guessed that nothing of worth had ever been sold in such a place. It was cheap, everything about it was poor, her father had not been able to think beyond the poverty which had been about their family for as long as she could remember.

Shona wandered through the place and she thought of her father half planning it but as ever too eager to begin. How must he have suffered when he could not make it pay because beyond everything he still had a market trader's way about him and would not be able to talk anybody into helping, into loaning him money, into going into the venture with him, into selling furniture or china or quality clothes if he had even got as far as that.

She went upstairs but the further rooms were just as dismal except that there was nothing in them and never had been whereas downstairs there was the odd piece of old furniture, various boxes, tables and chairs to display whatever goods had been on sale. Then she moved along to the part of the building which her father had obviously seen as living quarters.

They were cold and empty but she could see what he had intended and she was amazed at his ideas. The rooms all had fireplaces in them and there was a big kitchen and a dining room and a sitting room and various bedrooms. He must have thought that he would employ many people in his shop and that they would live here, he had not seen this place as the second-hand goods shop it had been, he wanted a department store. For the first time ever it seemed to her that she felt sympathy for him, his vision had not been recognized.

She went out the back of the building to see what lay beyond the yard and there were outbuildings and in them she discovered a huge supply of coal and wood and her heart lifted. She would be able to stay here. Aidan Hedley had not said that she could not and while she was sure that strictly speaking she should not she had nowhere else to go, she certainly didn't want to spend her money on lodgings.

This brought her to other practicalities. She had had nothing to eat for days so she locked up the front of the shop and trudged across the Market Place and went down into the indoor market.

It was as exciting and varied as she remembered and all kinds of goods were on sale, cheese in big yellow and white rounds, fish glistening, silver hams hanging from the ceiling, butter golden, and there was also the smell of pies, beef, low and wide, pork high and hot with juice, sandwiches, beef and horseradish. She bought a hot pork pie and devoured it in the shadows, she was hungry for the first time since James had died and the pie was good. She licked her fingers afterwards and then she bought more sensible things like tea and milk and bread and carrots, leeks and parsnips and barley and a piece of ham for soup and split peas in a muslin bag and then some cleaning equipment, a mop and bucket, disinfectant, vinegar to clean the windows and polish and cloths. Then she bought a teapot and a kettle and some cheap crockery and cutlery and a big pan and a smaller one and a big knife and matches.

It was almost dark by then. She bought candles and hurried back to the shop and before it grew dark she had lugged up the two flights of stairs coal and wood, there were various papers which helped to light the kitchen stove.

She found how to turn on the water and within minutes she was able to make tea, and by the light from two candles she cleaned the kitchen as best she could while the stove warmed up. She made broth and took comfort from the smell as it cooked. She closed the door so that the room would warm and she sat by the stove and had the soup with bread with chunks of ham and pease pudding and she began to feel better.

She slept on the floor in her coat. It was uncomfortable but she had not slept at all the night before and she was beyond caring. She awoke, stiff in the dawn, to find that the stove had almost gone out so she put more coal on to it, made tea and had tea and bread for breakfast.

Then she put on her coat and ventured outside. The day was milder than it had been the day before and she walked down and across Elvet Bridge and up Church Street to St Oswald's where her father would be buried, one of the few memories of her childhood was her mother holding her hand and the church seeming so big and the singing.

The grass was wet and her father's stone was not difficult to find because it had been there only a few months. She paused in front of it, there was nothing on it but his name and dates but it was an expensive marble stone. If the city had had to pay for this then surely they would not have done such a thing. She stood there until she was chilled and then she walked back to town and called in at the solicitor's and asked politely whether Mr Hedley had a few minutes and it seemed that he did because she was ushered into his office and to her surprise he said to her, 'Can I take you to lunch?'

She stared at him. Was this what solicitors did? She had no money to speak of.

'Well, I – I'm not—'

'How about the little cafe in Silver Street?'

That didn't sound too grand, so not knowing why, she agreed and off they went.

Shona had not been in an eating place with a man for years and he was so efficient, politely insisting on a table by the window, offering her the menu, and she was hungry. She ventured to ask him what he intended to have and when the reply was steak and chips she opted to have the same.

'I wanted to ask you something,' she said and she realized that he had known that and it was the very reason he had asked her here and she thought it very shrewd of him.

He looked enquiringly at her.

'By all means,' he said.

There was nobody near, the little tables were set well apart and she thought he had brought her here on purpose because it was informal.

'Who paid for my father's funeral?'

He looked slightly disconcerted.

'I went to the graveyard this morning,' she said. 'He has an expensive headstone.'

Aidan hesitated. 'Harry Darling.'

Shona caught at her breath. There was silence during which Aidan Hedley looked out of the window as though he was not sure what to say.

'Your father died outside Mr Darling's bank. Mr Darling was there, tried to help him.'

The sleet began and they sat and watched it and it was a distraction, it somehow filled up the way that they did not talk.

The food came, Shona's appetite was gone but she made herself eat because it would have been rude to leave it. They drank tea and then he said, 'Have you any plans?'

'None.'

'I thought you might be returning to Northumberland and that perhaps you would wish me to put the shop on the market.'

'Do I owe you money, Mr Hedley, for your work?'

'No.' He spoke lightly.

'Harry Darling paid.'

'He did.'

'He lives in Durham or nearby?'

'He owns the bank here in the Market Place and a good many others.'

She decided to be frank. What had she to lose?

'My husband died and I have nothing to go back to Northumberland for. I would like to stay at the shop and try to think what I could do next. Do you think that would be possible, considering the legalities?'

'I'm sorry to hear about your husband, Mrs Rainbow. I'm sure that you can do what you like with the building because now that you are here the legal process will be able to go through and end and I don't foresee any problems, the will is perfectly straightforward.'

When he had gone back to his office, assuring her that if there was anything more he could do for her he would be glad to help, Shona was inclined to go into the stout stone building which she saw was just across the way from her shop and shout at Harry Darling for what he had done but she didn't. He might have become the kind of man who wanted repayment and she didn't want to spend the money she had on such things.

Instead she went to the auction rooms, which were located in Elvet. The place was crowded as there was to be an auction that afternoon and she regarded that as luck while she looked around at the various items on sale.

She bought a bed complete with mattress and a big kitchen table with half a dozen chairs though she wasn't quite sure why, one chair would have done. She bought a sofa and a rug to go in front of the fire and afterwards she went to a shop in town and bought bedlinen and blankets and pillows and towels.

She spent one more night on the floor but the following morning the auction rooms delivered her goods and though the men grumbled about having to carry everything up two floors she was pleased when it was all in place and she was able to make up the bed and sit on the sofa by the fire in the room she had decided would be the living room.

It was not a big room, she wanted to be warm and cosy, and that night she was much happier, able to go to bed in comfort, eat at a table and be glad that she had somewhere to stay and it was hers, nobody was going to come and throw her out.

The following day therefore she got up with an excitement about her, something she had not experienced before. She bought more cleaning materials, a ladder and a long brush for the cobwebs.

It took her several days to clean the shop from top to bottom and by then she had decided that it needed new paint and that scared her. She had very little money left and no idea of how to make any. She ate nothing but vegetable soup and bread and drank nothing but tea and somehow the days went by quickly because she had discovered that she had enthusiasm for the shop, she liked the place, it was nothing to do with her father, she told herself.

She had been there for about four days when a man banged on the big double doors and seeing her busy came in. He was tall and dark and rather nice looking, Shona thought, he had a friendly intelligent face and was smiling at her.

'Good afternoon. I'm Ned Fleming. I own the local newspapers. Are you hoping to open up the old place?'

Shona looked doubtfully at him.

'I don't know,' she admitted, climbing down from the ladder where she had been painting. 'I'm Shona Rainbow. My father owned it, you see.'

'Might you plan to sell stationery? I could do you sale or return,' he offered.

Shona looked hard at his open face and thought they were the most wonderful words she had ever heard.

'You could have some stationery with the shop's name on it and desks where ladies can write notes and you could sell newspapers and periodicals and writing materials.

'I also do publishing and printing. If you want posters, leaflets, headed notepaper I could do all those and if you wanted to sell books I have several authors I publish now, popular fiction, it sells very well and many of the authors live in or around Durham and write about this area and about things which interest the local people.

'The women of the town like love stories and the younger ones like children's books. The men like a good mystery so we cater for everybody and this would be the perfect place to have book launches, it's so big,' he said, turning full circle in admiration.

It was the first time a man had put a business proposition to her. It was not exactly what she was looking for but it was a start and a buzz of excitement went through her head.

'I could also advertise for you in my newspapers. I have a dozen weeklies in the different villages around here and a daily of course and since you were selling my products I would do you a very good rate.'

A pretty woman stood in the doorway.

'There you are,' she accused him.

He turned around slowly as though he wanted to delay just a little because he enjoyed the anticipation and then he smiled at the figure partly blocking out the light.

'This is my wife, Annabel. Annabel runs the Ladies' Forum which comes out weekly and she is involved in all the newspaper ventures we have.'

He introduced them and Annabel asked about her plans and admired the place.

'Would you be interested in stocking the magazine?' Annabel Fleming said. 'I could write a piece about you setting up a big store, no woman has done such a thing anywhere as far as I know, certainly not around here. When are you planning to open?'

Shona hesitated. Ned Fleming looked at her and he smiled.

'Mrs Rainbow's Emporium,' he said.

Shona was confused for a few moments and then inspired by it. She had never come across people like the Flemings and she could feel a warm glow of excitement rising from the depths of her stomach as never before.

Shona had never thought she was anything like her father but she could sense the mulish quality. She wanted this, no matter what anybody said or thought. She could see in her mind the front of the building with big windows and lights inside and people buying Christmas presents and the name across the front.

'I could ask Susan Whitton to call,' Annabel offered. 'She runs the Silver Street cafe and might be able to help you out in all kinds of ways.'

Shona thanked her and when the Flemings had gone she set to work again, painting.

Shona made herself go to see Harry. She took all the courage that she had and ventured as far as the neat stone building which had the name Darling's Bank so improbably to her across the front, it was such an incongruous name for a bank. As soon as she went in she could see how orderly it was, hushed, the tellers on one side, each positioned behind a glass, standing, polite and ready to help, and at the other side several people behind desks with chairs at the front and there was a notice which said that the bank was happy to see people privately and appointments could be made to see the under-managers, Mr Trevors and Mr Edwards. There was nothing about the manager himself.

As she stood unsure a young man got up from behind one

of the desks, he was the only one who had nobody in front
of him talking and doing business and he came over to her,
asked if she had made an appointment.

'I want to see Mr Darling.'

'Mr Darling is very busy all week. Perhaps Mr Trevors would
do.'

'No.' She looked straight at him.

'Oh,' he said, surprised, she thought. 'Well, in that case I
could make you an appointment for some time next week.'

'My business with Mr Darling is personal and nothing to
do with the bank itself and I think he would see me if you
told him I was here. If he has someone with him I would be
glad to come back later.'

'Yes, of course,' the young man said, 'perhaps you could give
me your name and I will see what can be done,' and he smiled
at her in a way that she admired and she thought that Harry
trained his people very well.

She said who she was and he offered her a seat and he
disappeared into the gloom which led to the back of the
building. Very soon afterwards the young man came back,
trying to disguise his curiosity.

'Mr Darling will be glad to see you,' he said, 'please come
this way.'

She followed him into a wide hall and all the way down a
long corridor and at the end of it he opened a big oak door
and she was ushered into a large office. She barely recognized
the man who got up from behind the huge square leather-
topped desk. He was very well dressed in a quiet manner which
was so obviously meant to put other people at their ease that
she couldn't have described him.

You didn't notice his clothes, at least she wouldn't have if
it hadn't been for the fact that the last time she had seen him
he had been seventeen and had worn a very cheap suit and
was nothing more than a boy. That had all gone. He didn't
smile, he didn't hold out a hand to her. He just said softly, as
he got to his feet and came around the desk as though it was
an intrusion between them, 'Hello, Shona, how are you?'

'Hello, Harry.'

'Would you like to sit down?'

He waved a hand at a big leather chair, not the kind of thing she had imagined would grace a banker's office, it looked too informal, like something you could sink into after a hard day as somebody handed you a glass of something alcoholic, bubbly and light and totally luxurious and frivolous, which sat badly with her ideas of what banks and bank managers were like.

She remembered his hands, those long slender fingers rough from outdoor work and grubby, loading boxes on to market stalls in the dim light of early morning when the market was held on Thursday and Saturdays no matter what the weather.

'I just wanted to thank you for – for what you did for my father. I understand he died out here.' She paused, Harry said nothing, 'And you – you paid for everything. It must have cost you a great deal of money. I will pay you back when I can afford it.'

'There's no need,' Harry said largely. He really was so very quiet, and that was something entirely different about him. 'How's James?'

'He drowned at sea at the beginning of the month. That – that was when I found the solicitor's letter.'

Harry said, as he must, that he was very upset for her that James had died and she nodded, she had heard the same thing from other people, they felt obliged to say something rather than nothing.

And that was when she asked the question she really wanted to hear the answer to.

'Where did he get all the money from to buy that – that monstrosity of a place?'

Twelve

Harry had had no experience of other people's grief. He imagined that Tam would get used to Shona not being there but Tam would look for her as though he expected her to appear, as though at any minute she would remember her family obligations and come home. He clung to the idea, Harry could see, and at first he would not leave the house.

'She'll be back in a minute,' was the first way Tam handled it and Harry was obliged to leave him there while he went to get the horse and cart and then went off to the markets. He stopped handling the stalls himself and got another stall holder, Terry, to help him. Terry was the daughter of the ironmonger across the street and had had no job and he thought had needed one. He dealt with her father over things he wanted for the horse and cart and Terry seemed bored there, her father had three sons and although nobody seemed to realize she was surplus Harry saw it straight away and asked her if she would like to sell curtains for him and she agreed so fast that he had to slow her down.

'I'll talk to your dad about it.'

He knew he needed to do that as her father was the kind of man who ruled his family and expected them not to argue and at first he seemed to think it was a stupid idea.

'She's got enough to do here.'

Harry glanced around him. There was plenty of work but it was work for men, lifting and carrying and talking to the customers who were mostly men. Even in the office her father employed men.

Harry offered to pay her well and that did it. Some people's greed always bettered them and so he went to the girl and told her how much he would pay and she said, 'I don't want me dad to get his hands on it.'

'We'll put it in the bank,' Harry said and thought that finished it and he was glad he had employed her. She liked selling curtains, she was good at it as he had thought she would be and she blossomed, she smiled there because it was something she understood and was interested in, he would hear her talking about colour schemes to the various women, about how they wanted their front rooms to look and then she would lead them on to buying carpets and rugs and other things which Harry began to order for people to beautify their houses.

When he went to the banks however he was not surprised to discover that she couldn't have a bank account, she was too young and she was a woman, it had to be her father who had it and since this defeated Harry's object he had to think of something else. He had met and somehow got around similar problems with himself and Shona being so young and wanting to save money in a bank but this seemed different to him.

He came out of the bank, the third one he had been to, and wandered back towards the market stalls in the Market Place, it was one of his days in Durham, and he stood there and as he stood he saw a good big building. It had been a hotel but so disreputable of late that it was empty.

That afternoon, leaving the stalls in her now fairly experienced hands with a proviso that the others would help her if it got too much and they nodded, those within earshot because Harry had by then helped most of them with loans, he went to see his solicitor, Mr Jameson of Hedley, Jameson and Hedley and enquired as to whether he might view the shop and he saw it that very afternoon.

It was one of those lovely ugly buildings such as the early Victorians had thought up, it had big rooms and high ceilings, some monstrous ornamentation in stone on the outside but inside he thought it might do very well for what he wanted and although it was at present far too big the rent was something he could easily sustain while he worked out what he wanted to do. After his long look round, going from room to big room and gazing from the windows over the market square, he stood outside for a long time until he felt obliged to go back and assist as the market had become very busy.

When they closed up for the evening, however, he went back to Mr Jameson and told him that he would rent the building for an initial period of six months and then he went back and laughed at himself as he took the horse back to his stable, and talked long to him, since he was the only person who wanted to listen, and then slowly made his way home.

Tam had barely moved from his position by the long dead fire. In his enthusiasm for the idea of a new venture Harry had completely forgotten about him. Tam looked up and he even said, 'Shona?' and Harry realized that he had been sitting there expecting her back and that the hope which had dawned in his eyes died the moment he saw that it was Harry.

It was the first time that Harry had known Tam stay sober for more than two days. He was in shock, Harry could see. He didn't eat, he didn't sleep, he hardly moved at all in the days that followed. Harry made himself go to the market but now he was employing people every day to run the stalls as he took charge of his new premises.

It was hard too to do everything in the house. He had known that Shona did a great deal but it was only when there was no food, no clean clothes, no clean towels or sheets and the floor was sticky with dirt that he thought they should move to somewhere decent and employ someone to housekeep. Tam wouldn't go. Harry had known he wouldn't and it was impossible to move him and it was impossible to leave him and often he cursed Shona for her selfishness.

He took to doing the housework himself, to sending out the washing to a woman on the end of the row who did such things and to buying food, having got help with the horse and cart, though he did miss the private conversations with Julius.

Soon his days consisted of trying to persuade Tam to eat breakfast, leaving to check that other people were seeing to the goods being taken to the appropriate market and that the people employed were running the stalls and taking the right money and then going into the city to see how the premises were progressing as he was having some alterations made inside, nothing permanent of course just so that he could open soon.

It was a good day when they put up the sign outside and Harry had never been proud of himself until that moment. It read in discreet letters Darling's Bank.

His first customer was Terry. She didn't need to have her father's signature, she didn't need anybody to take responsibility for what she was doing. During the first few weeks Harry had intended to be at the bank for only an hour or so a day because the place was not ready to be opened but Terry had spoken to the other market people who had been borrowing from him for years and most of them did not trust banks but they trusted him.

They came to him to make deposits, for small loans and business advice, and right from the beginning Harry no longer had the time to work on the markets at all and he, Terry and the others found him new people to run his stalls for the first few weeks until he realized that there was no longer any point in his having a stake there, he made enough from what he was making with the bank for his small needs but then the needs changed as he knew they would.

He was still looking after Tam but Tam was no longer going to the pub. It was as though the shock of losing Shona altered his whole life. He would talk in the evenings of going for her and bringing her back. Several times Harry pointed out that they did not know where she was but Tam would rage over and over again about the man who had taken her away and how could she be so disloyal as to treat her father like this.

During the day while Harry was out he stayed at home. He came down with colds and the flu and could not have gone to the pub even if he had wanted and in the end Harry found a woman from further along, Mrs Frobisher, who would come in and clean and make a meal and for the money which Harry paid her was happy to sit there over the fire as the bad weather approached and talk to Tam.

She had no family, her husband had gone off years since and her only daughter was married, so every day she came to their house and it was a good arrangement, she kept an eye on Tam and cooked meals. Tam could no longer resist freshly baked bread with good butter and home-made plum jam and Harry would come back to find them sitting together eating tea and she would stay after that if Harry had business to attend to because he was finding everything too much to do at first but by the time he had given his market pitches to other people and sorrowfully parted with the horse and cart to the green-grocer and his daughters and given over the housekeeping to

Mrs Frobisher there should have been less to do but somehow there wasn't.

He needed to take on help at the bank. It wasn't a case of it being officially opened, it was just that from the first day when people saw the doors ajar because of the workmen, they came in. Harry was so well known now for his good sense and good ideas that the small-business people from the area came to him as they would trust no other banker.

It was Christmas when Tam finally walked into the bank. Harry was employing two other people part time by then and he was ushered through into the room Harry had chosen for his office.

'Didn't expect to see me, eh?' Tam looked around him. 'You're doing all right for yourself? You wouldn't have got far without my lass.'

Harry didn't reply, it was true of course, he would have died in the snow if Shona had not saved him, but just at that point he did not particularly want to be reminded of it since he was trying not to think about her, it would do him no good.

'Have I got much money?' Tam said next. He looked straight at Harry as though Harry was trying to do him out of something. Harry had seen that look before though not directly at him.

'You have a considerable amount, in spite of everything.'

'In spite of me drinking, is that what you mean?'

Harry didn't say anything to that. For years now he had put what he thought of as Tam's fair share into an account.

'It's grown with you leaving it in the bank.'

'How does it do that?'

'Well, the bank manager lends it out to other people and charges interest and puts it into other things, at least I will.' He hadn't actually got as far as investment. He had made sure that the important money was in other people's banks, those who knew what they were doing with investment until he did. He had seen a house that day, just a small one he thought he might renovate and rent out, and some shop premises in Claypath which showed promise and there were other places, other ventures he could put money into.

'I've seen a place I want, a shop, you know the big place

across the street from here. I've always liked it, always wanted it. Can I afford it?'

The place he meant was enormous and it was at the moment a collection of small shops but Harry could see what he meant, it would make one very big store, a wonderful idea, but he didn't have time for such a thing or enough interest and he had no faith at all in the idea that Tam could sustain even a week in any job.

'Why would you want to do that? The way you live costs you nothing.' Harry was paying for everything. 'You won't move into something bigger and better—'

'Aye, now that you're somebody you don't like coming from Paradise Lane,' Tam scoffed. 'You don't have to stay there, I don't know why you do. I don't need you, I never needed you.'

This was so obviously not true that Harry didn't say anything.

'The only person who ever mattered to me was her,' Tam said. 'She was my whole world. For her to throw herself away on that lad, I can't imagine why she did it. Running away like that as though she didn't care any more. Well, she won't find better. So how much money have I got?'

Harry didn't want to tell him, it was by now a substantial amount, but he had to, it was Tam's money after all. So he told him. The old man swelled with pride even though he had made little of it, being in the pub most of the past few years, Harry making sure that what would have been his share was looked after.

'I can buy the place then, turn it into summat grand, a sort of alternative for them folk who runs the market and the indoor market too, summat better.'

'You think there's a need for it?'

'I must do, mustn't I, or I wouldn't ask. So, I'll have me money please. By Friday.' Tam got up. 'And there's another thing, I want you out of my house, I don't need you there and you can tell that Frobisher woman I don't need her there either. I'm not paying her to sit over my fire.'

'You should think about all this.'

'I have thought about it. I want you out and I want my brass. I never liked you, coming in and interfering. She would never have left if there'd just been her and me.'

He went and Harry reflected that you always needed some-body else to blame when you could no longer bear who you were. And maybe he was wrong, maybe now that Tam didn't drink, now that time had passed, he might manage something, he might turn the place across the street into something fine.

It certainly needed it, he had been thinking about it himself, but it was too big a venture and he wanted to get more involved in banking and not so much in shopkeeping. He wished he could turn Tam from this course, he didn't think there was a need for such a place but Tam so obviously did not want advice from somebody he saw as no more than a young lad and Harry knew that he wouldn't take any notice.

He had thought that he wanted to leave but one's idea of leaving a place and actually doing it were so different that Harry was surprised. It was as though he was leaving Shona, he knew that it was a stupid idea but he couldn't help how his memory offered him so many days and nights of her with the fear that when he left he would leave all those behind.

Also he had never lived alone and he had existed in several places before he reached the sanctuary of Shona and Paradise Lane so that he had to force himself from the house. He had nothing to leave beyond a few books and clothes and he called himself sentimental that the bedroom still had two beds in it and he looked over before he walked out of the bedroom and down the stairs for the last time and he could see himself lying in the snow so many years ago now.

And then he thought of how many nights he had lain there since she had gone, thinking of her and looking across and wishing it was the early days. He had been happy then for the first time in his life and none of it could be recalled to his satisfaction. Memories were not enough.

She was, he knew it now, the only person he had ever loved, the only person he would be happy to spend time with every day of his life, to eat an evening meal with her, drink wine and just be there.

Nobody else held his attention in that way though he had looked, sought, hoped that someone else would. She had been the sole light in his life and she had gone. He was as badly off as Tam in some ways and he thought of Tam again and whether it was worth trying to talk him out of this foolish venture but he knew it was no use, Tam had been jealous of the way that Shona had cared for him.

Tam wanted to be the only person that Shona ever cared for. None of it was reasonable, none of it was generous or commendable in any way, and Harry wished so much that he could feel like that again with somebody else. Having something like that once was to know loneliness, emptiness when it was over, and he envied James Rainbow as he had envied no one before because Shona so obviously felt the same about James.

He lingered in the little house in Paradise Lane but only because Tam was not there. He had worried in case Tam went to the pub but the pub had now become the building, or the other way round, one obsession had been another, it was not the drink, it was the idea, it was the holding of attention which Tam needed and he had found another place where he could exist without Shona. Who was Harry to deprive him of it?

He had no idea where he should go. He had nobody to go to, nobody cared about him. Everybody liked him but nobody was family, nobody expected to be needed or wanted outside of working hours. In the end, it seemed ludicrous but he turned up at the County Hotel and after his first amazement at himself for what seemed like a stupid idea he was rather pleased with himself.

He asked for what he assumed was a fairly modest room and carried his one suitcase to it with little expectation but he had to remind himself when he reached it that the only place he had lived in for years was the awful little house in Paradise Lane.

This was luxury indeed by comparison and he wanted to laugh because he had assumed that the person on the desk did not know him, that it would be nothing special, and then he caught a glimpse of himself in the mirror and saw how well cut his suit was. He hadn't intended it to be but he knew the local tailor, had loaned him money recently to expand his business, and even though the suit had not been expensive it was of good cloth and well cut and he was young and – he laughed again and then he opened the doors and stepped out on to his balcony which overlooked the river.

He stood there in the bitter cold for a few moments and then went back inside. A big fire burned in the grate and there was a huge bed and there were great big wardrobes and a dressing table and a writing desk and chair and a sofa in the corner. The carpet was thick and the walls were delicately papered with improbable blue birds with a pale cream background which looked similar to the kind of curtains Shona had once sold on the market. He rid himself of the image and then thought that he would go down to dinner, he had booked himself a meal in the restaurant.

Harry had thought he did not care much about food but the idea was dispelled that evening because for the first time in his life he had a choice in a restaurant like this and he chose well and he liked sitting by himself with the cold night now raining against the windows and he was eating trout and then chicken and a delicious chocolate pudding and cheese and he drank wine and finished with brandy and coffee in the sitting room beside the window which looked out over the river and when he was sufficiently tired he went upstairs.

He tried to feel guilty about spending his money so freely but couldn't, he had never done such a thing before and he was enjoying himself. It did occur to him and had when he entered the dining room that people were looking at him and it seemed that this was no bad thing, if he could live well then he must be doing well and perhaps they would put their money into his bank and if they didn't he didn't much care now that he was drinking his brandy. It tasted so wonderful, so thick and sweet, and caught at the back of his throat not too much in a reassuringly expensive way.

He went to bed almost happy. In his absence his fire had been attended to, the bed turned down, the curtains pulled to against the night and though he had not asked for it there was a decanter of brandy and a glass and some ratafia biscuits on the little table, discreetly to one side. There was hot water too. Harry could not take in the elegance of it all, he sat by the fire for a while and then he undressed and washed and got into bed and it was the most wonderful bed he had ever been in, it was possibly, he thought, as he fell asleep, the most wonderful bed in the whole world.

Thirteen

Shona left Harry's bank. She tried to slow down her footsteps and to take leave of him without flight, without thinking, but it was not easy. She must go past the people in the front office and this she did slowly, realizing that he had not followed her out, indeed why would he?

By the time she got back to the shop she was crying and remembering what life had been like in Paradise Lane and that Harry had gone back there probably for the first time since he had escaped, whenever that was, to find her father's will and then he had seen that Tam Hardy was buried and properly with a golden stone and his name etched there like he was respected, loved.

She thought of Harry getting down beside her father in the market square when he collapsed. Was that what had happened?

Did he look across the market square from his fine building and watch while her father spent every penny that he had accumulated in those dark times on something which would be no good or had he kept the whole thing away from him with his business and his politeness?

Aidan Hedley had said that the building had been empty for years. She thought of her father failing yet again and so badly – she could not believe that anybody could be so stupid, so obsessed, so driven that they would buy something and then not have anything left to carry it through and yet she pitied her father because he had seen his dream die and after that he had fallen on to the cobbles outside Harry's office and it had all ended there in the cold rain across the street from where the building stood. Had it seemed to mock him, had it been the last thing her father had seen or had he taken in Harry's face and would that have been any better, with Harry's supposedly comforting words ringing in his ears like a litany of guilt?

She was working with the doors open the following

morning. It was a bright morning, colder inside than out so the morning let in the warmth and the bright sunshine.

The owner of the Silver Street cafe, Susan Whitton, stood in the doorway.

'I hear you're setting up in competition,' she said.

Mrs Whitton was a formidable woman but Shona looked straight at her and said, 'I was going to come and see you. It's not going to be competition, I want you to make the food, at least start off with simple things, that can be reheated. Will you take a look?'

Susan was shown the ovens and the cafe as it was. It had come on in some ways, it was pretty. The walls were white and the tables were covered in blue cloths and she had found yellow and blue crockery cheaply in the market and got it for a cut-down price and the old dining chairs which did not match Shona had painted in white.

Susan clucked her teeth over the inadequacy of the ovens and then she looked around. 'I like the piano, it's good to have music when you can find someone to play.'

Shona liked the piano too. Somehow it had survived and she was having it tuned with the idea of using it if it was good enough to play.

'You'll need a waitress, at least one, and somebody to man the ovens,' Susan said.

'That's a lot of people to pay.'

'This is the trouble. You might have to do a good many things yourself until you can afford more.'

While Shona was having a cup of tea later in the day there was a noise from the main part of the front shop, somebody was shouting, a man with a thick accent. Shona got up to see who it was and a small dark young man with black eyes and an olive skin was standing there.

'I am looking for work. You are starting some business here?'

'I cannot employ anyone.'

He was nothing much more than a boy and he had left Italy because his family was so poor that they could not support him. He had made his way here and now he had nowhere to stay.

'What can you do?' she said.

'Everything.'

This, Shona thought, was desperation but she took him in and he set to and swept the floors. Later he talked Shona into giving him a little money (she half thought she might not see him again after that) and he went off to the market across the way and came back with flour, cheap meat and a few vegetables. That evening he made for them the most delicious meal that Shona had ever eaten. It was little parcels which he seemed to conjure up, stuffed with minced meat.

A few days later she said nothing when he did not offer to help. He had slept the night on her only sofa – she had locked her bedroom door, just in case – and was awake and out of the shop early and he still had some of the money she had given him from the day before. She wanted to give him a chance, to see what he could do without insisting he do what she wanted.

He came back with a large pan he had bought in the market and several mysterious packages and spent the day in the kitchen and Shona kept coming back and found that he was making toffee and then fudge. When it was done he put it into small see-through bags with a twist tied with a little piece of ribbon and these he sold to the passers-by just outside the front door of the shop, coming back gleefully to Shona that evening with the money he had made.

That night he insisted on cooking again and the money made from the sweets meant that he went off once again to the market and they ate well again.

The following day he made peppermints and dipped them in chocolate and chocolate truffles and other sweets, black and white with a hint of liquorice, and every day after that when the shop was closed the smell from the tiny kitchen wafted through the shop as he tended his preserving pans and twisted and turned the mixture and cut it into squares or dropped it into cold water. He began to branch out and to make the sweets which were popular with children and adults and she realized that he had been around various shops and done some research even though he had said nothing.

There was cinder toffee which was her personal favourite,

the sweet sticky almost sour smell was wonderful. He made various kinds of chocolate and with nuts or with candied fruit.

He made pink and white sugar mice, shaping the mice from fondant, but the best of all were the chocolate rabbits which he made from second-hand moulds he had found in an old shop beyond the Market Place in Fowlers Yard. The rich women of the town came and bought the mice and the rabbits, wrapped in pink ribbons. Gino, pressed by Shona, charged more for these than for anything but they took time to make and he could sell as many as he made.

The bad weather meant that the confectionery department moved a little further away from the doors and Shona set up more of the inside of the shop as she went along, she established it beside the cafe, and once she could see people coming in to buy the sweets she opened the cafe, and a widow with two half-grown children, Nancy Hobson, came to the door and asked Shona to take her in.

'We've nowhere to go and the weather is growing bad. We'll do all we can to help,' so Shona set Nancy on heating pastries and making tea and coffee and the two girls served in the cafe and kept the fires burning.

The Silver Street cafe supplied the food, Susan sent a selection every day and Shona was able to pay what she owed even from the first week.

Beds were bought for upstairs and fires were lit and in the kitchen now there were five people for Gino to cook for each evening. Shona acquired a big table and benches for her growing company. Nancy and her children had a room to themselves and the girls would go off to bed almost dropping with tiredness but they were not unhappy, they had food and warmth and good beds and it was more, Nancy said, than they had had in a long time.

The following day Shona went off to see Ned and found him in his shabby tiny office in Saddler Street. Ned never looked like a newspaper proprietor, rather as somebody who had just happened in, his tie askew and his trousers grubby no matter how well turned out he might be first thing in the morning. Annabel said that Ned collected dirt like other people collected stamps.

'I need a name for my sweets,' Shona told him and then she explained that she wanted something which could be threaded with the ribbon for the bags of confectionery which Gino was offering to the public. 'And I need a painter to put up the sign over the door.'

Ned printed Rainbow's Sweets so that each bag could be identified and he found her somebody to paint the sign. On the first dry day everything was arranged and Shona went out in the evening and looked happily at the black lettering with white behind it and above it all he had placed a rainbow and it read in big letters Mrs Rainbow's Emporium.

Fourteen

Some time since, Jason Taylor had come to Harry's office at the bank. For years now Harry had dreamed that he would, had even willed it when he had first gone into business, but now it didn't matter. He had come to the conclusion that nothing mattered but the day-to-day work and the fact that he could go back to the hotel each evening and have some peace. He spent his evenings alone, he had few friends, nor wanted them. He could walk from the County to his work.

At weekends he would go to the bank as usual and enjoy the peace and quiet. He normally got more done on Saturdays and Sundays than he did the rest of the week but that gave him lots of time for the inevitable interruptions, for the unscheduled meetings which he found it necessary to call and for him to fit in visits to all his banks in the area, often without letting them know so that they became used to surprise visits. It kept everybody alert and enabled him to think about the alteration of old buildings the better to suit what their use was now and the construction of new ones.

Jason Taylor had asked for the appointment several days before so Harry was not surprised to see him. The talk among local bankers was that Jason was badly in debt.

Harry didn't have to see him but he had decided that he would before making up his mind what to do and when Miss Piers announced Mr Taylor he got up, greeting him by name and smiling, holding out his hand and it was only then that he remembered how much at one time he had wanted Mr Taylor to come to him in need and all the hatred of him came back in such a way that Harry had to sit down abruptly. His guest had already taken a seat by then and didn't notice. Harry felt sick.

The man had got fatter and more red-faced since the last time they had met but he had been as repulsive as he could be to Harry when he was young. There was a tiny part of

Harry's mind willing to gamble that Jason Taylor would remember him, see the boy in his face, but he also knew that men do not remember children, even those they abuse. He saw his own face in the mirror beyond Taylor and scarcely recognized himself in the banker's hard dark eyes, sheer black hair and rather paler than usual face. Where had the poor half-starved skinny boy gone? There was nothing of him left.

Mr Taylor looked older than his years, no doubt excess of drink, meat and little boys' company had worked against him.

Harry listened to what the man said, he needed money to buy another business property, another shop.

Jason's reputation was as a good man and a good old-fashioned businessman. It was not his fault that he was losing money, they said, it was the times, the overseas markets, the way that wages had risen, the rising cost of materials everywhere, and people seemed not to know the intimacies of his former life.

Why should they, and even if they suspected that he had what was called 'led a wild youth' such things were admired and people did not understand what form self-indulgence often took. As with many men he hid, hopefully out of shame, that he could not stop himself for the way that he liked the feel and taste of young flesh. Harry was feeling so sick by now that he had to stop himself running from his own office and throwing up. The man in front of him was serious-faced and was going into detail about what he would do, how he would expand, all the other departments he could use with the rest of the space, it was an opportunity but he would need a loan.

Miss Piers brought in coffee. Harry was obliged to pretend that he wanted some and even to take a sip or two but the sickness was coming at him in waves so he tried not to think but to concentrate on what the man was saying.

'I'm hoping to buy the premises that Mr Hardy has left. I understand he has a daughter who lives at some distance and has lived there for a good many years and would probably not want to come back here so I thought that when she makes contact I will talk to Mr Hedley and see what can be done.'

'Really?'

'I can't afford the competition of another department store

and I have heard rumours that various shop-owners from other places are thinking they might buy it.'

'How would you back up the loan?'

'I have the other store.'

'It isn't making any money.'

'It does usually but I can't afford the competition of another store almost directly across the market square or it won't make any money at all,' Jason pointed out. 'I could always sell it on for some other form of business but at present I have to make sure that nobody betters me.'

He pushed across the desk the accounts he had brought with him.

Harry didn't have to see the books, he knew how little money the department store took. Jason Taylor paid his shop assistants as sparingly as he could, they worked long hours and there had been rumours lately that some of the goods were faulty, badly made or expensive.

It was not necessarily true, nor did it make him a worse employer than many others, and the fact that he was never at the store made him a gentleman to some people and not a bad manager which was what Harry thought him. Harry didn't shop there, he didn't shop anywhere, his tailor came to see him, his shoes were handmade by an expert in Newcastle and he didn't need anything else. If he had to buy something for anyone else he delegated the job to Miss Piers.

'Will you be able to give me a loan?' Jason Taylor asked.

'I would have to set the loan against your house.'

He looked appealingly at Harry. 'My wife and daughter love it.'

Harry was sure they did, so had his grandfather and presumably so did all the St Clairs who had lived on that site for so long.

Harry didn't know the Taylors socially and had always refused their efforts to entice him to their dinner parties. He didn't think he could ever go back to Dragon's Field.

'We haven't been there long, you know. We aren't like other people, able to trace our family home back hundreds of years. It is a beautiful house. I bought it before I married, I used to have wonderful parties there and then I married and Elspeth was born and brought up there. It belonged before that to a very fine family, the St Clairs. When the last of them died the place was left, when I bought it the family debts were paid off and we were able to move in.'

'Was there no heir?'

Mr Taylor looked surprised.

'Nobody at all, I understand,' he said.

Harry thought that Mr Taylor was speaking the truth and Harry was usually a good judge of men and he thought at least it was one thing he could not accuse Jason Taylor of, he had not deliberately taken the house from the St Clairs, he had not been aware of the boy, perhaps no one had been aware of him. There had been no pictures of his parents and when he had asked about them his grandfather had not wanted to talk and somehow he had gained the idea that they had run off, that they were not good people but his grandfather cared and that had been sufficient then.

'The debts must have been very big.'

'They were. The house was in a very bad way. I spent a great deal of money on repairs, too much really. I fell in love with the house, you see. There's something very special about it.' He laughed just a little. 'Have you ever heard the phrase "beyond here there be dragons"?

'Five hundred years ago where knowledge of map-making ran out, where the world stopped that was what was said, dragons lived on the edge of the world, where people were afraid to go beyond, the very idea that what you don't know anything about can terrify you. Local tales say that the bones of dragons were found there, they were most likely dinosaurs but I like the idea that dragons once lived there. Some people believe that they still exist and are in hiding.'

'What a nice idea,' Harry said stiffly.

'We have gargoyles on the outside of the house which are like small dragons.'

Harry almost said, 'I know,' and had to stop himself.

'I would not put my house up for mortgage if there was any way at all I could do this differently.'

'I'm afraid it's the only thing you have to gamble with,' Harry said.

Mr Taylor tried to smile.

'I never heard a banker talk of gambling,' he said.

'Oh but it is, like every other game.'

Mr Taylor seemed taken aback, shaken, and the room was silent before he said with a sigh, 'Very well then. If there is no other way.'

Harry agreed to loan him the money. Mr Taylor's face filled with relief and when the meeting ended he was shaking Harry warmly by the hand and thanking him so profusely and asking him to dinner and for once, Harry, caught off guard, said that he would.

When Mr Taylor had gone Miss Piers came in and the look on her face was of astonishment.

'Mr Taylor tells me you're going to his house for dinner on Saturday. I shall make a note of this in your diary.'

Harry wanted to tell her that he was unlikely to forget it but he couldn't. He tried to put the matter from his mind and all that day until halfway through the evening he concentrated on work because he could not bear to consider his own stupidity in having agreed to go back to a place that he had sworn he would never touch again and yet he knew very well that he had deliberately placed himself into such an awkward position that he would feel obliged to go. He must see the place that haunted him and be free from that haunting. He must face what frightened him, even in that place where there were dragons.

That night as he sat on the balcony outside his room at the hotel, drinking his coffee black and thinking back over his day, his face, though he didn't know it, registered other emotions when he pictured in his mind the dining room with its oak-panelling damage where Taylor and his cronies shot for sport when they were young.

There had been a long table where naked women would lie drunk among apples, oranges and pears, to be taken like food. The men would be so drunk that their breath stank of wine, half-eaten food was thrown to him as it was to the dogs which had retreated to the corners. The servants would knock him aside because they couldn't see him there in the shadows, when all the lighting was candles and fire, the men playing cards, the women singing and he being lifted from one to another when he was quite small, to be petted and caressed and to return the favour when asked.

He willed himself not to think any further, not to dwell on the darkness and the cold and the loneliness, on the sudden bright lights and how he could be sick from food because he had gone without for so long and then hands on him and being used for other people's pleasure, being hurt and being completely alone and not mattering at all, as though you weren't human, you weren't regarded as such. He had learned not to speak because no one listened, nobody cared. It seemed to amuse them too that you might protest, that you might cry, that you might call out, that—

Harry sipped hot coffee and forced the images from his mind and made himself remember the early days at Dragon's Field with his grandfather and was surprised to discover that they did not please him either, no parents, no friends, nobody but an old man who it seemed had ruined the last of his family's chances of any future and Harry of any security or peace of mind or self-respect that he might know.

And it seemed to him then that Taylor was right, nobody knew of him except the servants and they wouldn't care. Nobody thought that there was anybody of any importance in the house since his grandfather went nowhere and saw no one. He thought of how Jason Taylor had said that day that he had bought the place and paid the family debts but why was it that nobody had ever thought about the child or cared that they might try for some kind of future on his behalf?

Going back to the house that Saturday evening was one of the hardest things Harry had ever done but he was not surprised to discover that the place was so altered that he would not have known it. Jason Taylor, though Harry did not wish to acknowledge it, had been a very young man then, careless and stupid. He was not that any more, he had married and produced a child and his reputation for wild parties was forgotten. He was just another businessman.

The house was so very beautiful, that was a surprise. He could not go back there with anything other than hatred and resentment so strong that he felt he could have killed Jason Taylor had a weapon been available but he wished very much that it had been as it was when he was an abused child there, he did not want the house to look so normal, he had not realized until that moment how much he hated every room.

Since Jason Taylor had married it had changed very much. Mrs Taylor had been a society beauty and she had come from a good local family. Introduced to her now for the first time Harry was not surprised that Taylor had wanted her. She had bright blonde hair and blue eyes and milky skin and a figure that needed no improvement but had it anyway in a very expensive blue gown.

She wore diamonds around her neck and Harry was aware that Jason Taylor had needed the loan from his bank very much indeed because he was living beyond his means. His wife and child seemed unaware of it, as any decent man would not tell them, but Harry was beginning to doubt that the loan would cover all the expenses and the buying of Shona's premises even though they were in bad repair and had been left so long.

'I was beginning to think you would never accept an invitation to dinner, Mr Darling, and we would never meet.'

He said all the right things and then their daughter came in and Harry nearly fell over. He had heard how lovely Elspeth Taylor was but he could not help gazing at her. She smiled so naturally that Harry took to her straight away, he would have imagined that any daughter of Jason Taylor's would be a spoiled brat in over-elaborate clothes, thinking much of herself, but she was not, she greeted him with obvious pleasure and slight shyness and did not do the dreadful thing that women so often did, changing the subject to suit whatever was his wish.

It was just the four of them but even so it could have been a banquet, the wine was the best he had ever tasted, the food as well, though he ate and drank sparingly and it was not from any fault of the evening, it was just that he remembered the evenings in this dining room where he had been part of the meal in a sense.

He tried to remember better days but couldn't bring any to mind. He tried to make conversation but the effort was terrible. Coming back here made his mind relive again all the awful hours he had spent here. When the meal was over several men turned up, the women went off into another room and the cards came out and Harry froze. The card tables were set up and he was invited to play.

'I don't play cards.'

Mr Taylor looked anxious. He realized he had committed a faux pas. 'Oh,' he said, 'I'm so sorry, I didn't know.'

Before anything more could be said one of the other men who was not much older than himself, Ned Fleming, who owned the local newspapers, got up at once and said, 'Mr Darling's right, it bores some of us. How about we go into the library and have a glass of port together?'

Harry had known Fleming already, had originally been ready to dislike the way that he immediately took over, but he knew by now that Ned was confident and educated and Ned looked straight at him so he agreed.

Ned Fleming was coal rich but didn't live at his family's mansion in the city with his father but in a tiny terraced house with his pretty southern wife and his baby. He ran newspapers which the working people enjoyed. People called him a socialist for it but Ned didn't seem to mind.

With a glass in his hand and Ned offering Taylor's cigars, Harry was given to say, 'Thanks.'

'Not at all. I can't think of anything I want to do less than play cards but I've had a long day and Annabel is at her mother's.'

'How's the newspaper world?' was all that Harry needed to say and Ned was off on his favourite subject and Harry liked any kind of business talk and was quite happy there for the next two hours and when it was time to leave Ned said in an offhand way, 'Call in at the newspaper office some time if you fancy it and we could have a drink after work.' He left it at that so Harry would feel no obligation and Harry was very pleased to have met him again and liked how casual Ned was and yet there was something companionable about it and relaxed. It made him think about the first time he had gone to their house for dinner and how fond of them both he had become.

Fifteen

Harry had liked the little house in Sutton Street where Ned and Annabel Fleming lived until they moved to the house which Ned's father had bought. They had dared to have dinner parties there, they called them 'supper' and the first one he was invited to had occurred when Ned casually one Wednesday morning at the bank said to him, 'Why don't you come and have supper with us on Saturday? Annabel would love to meet you properly.'

Harry had no idea how you turned down such an invitation so casually delivered. He was not used to it. People treated him with care and he knew that when he was asked to the houses of the well-off people in the area it was only because of who he had become.

Behind his back he knew that people called him 'a gutter-snipe' and he rarely went anywhere because of that but also because the prosperous women of the city cared that he was rich and unmarried and were not above seating their unmarried daughters at either side of him at dinner and the daughters were not above smiling and agreeing with him over every possible subject so that Harry could think of nothing to say and was known as difficult.

He went to their little terraced house and was aghast to find Annabel alone, in the smallest house he had been in since he had left Paradise Lane. His hostess was flushed from cooking, had flour on her face and pulled off her apron as he entered. They had met before but only at a party and he had not spoken to her beyond politeness and he had admired her beauty, her lovely voice and the fact that she was in business with her husband and well liked in the district but he had been unprepared for her to call him by his first name, when they barely knew one another, and say, 'Oh, Harry, thank God for you. Here, sit down and take Thomas. He's too big for me to carry around while I'm cooking and I have to see to the oven.'

Harry, dumped in the nearest chair with a whimpering child, was rather taken aback at first but the smells from Annabel's kitchen were so wonderful that it was difficult not to be happy.

The child fell asleep and when she once again had time to turn and give Thomas her attention it was to announce, 'What a genius you are, he never does that with people he doesn't know well,' and Harry was proud to think that the first time he had held a small child had been so successful.

She took Thomas from him but instead of delivering the child upstairs and out of the way she merely put him on to a sofa which stood in the shadows at the back of the room and then she put cushions around him so that he would not fall and came back and poured red wine generously into huge glasses so that it caught at the lamplight and glowed and as she did so her husband came in and they sat about and talked and Harry realized that he was to be the only guest, that he had been asked here for no professional reason or for who he was or even to meet a woman, he was there because they wanted his company.

Happiness was alien to him, contentment he only just recognized that evening. Annabel had made a stew and there was bread with it and afterwards a rhubarb crumble, nothing was ornate or fanciful but it was one of the best evenings of Harry's life.

He was sorry when the Flemings moved into a big house on the edge of town, Black Well Tower. He had not been invited there yet, he hoped jealously that nobody else had either. He did not want the Flemings to become grand.

So he hesitated when the invitation to dinner arrived.

This was no casual invitation such as they had always been. He didn't want to go there and have it be as other dinner parties had, everyone wearing their best clothes and their very best manners. Perhaps the Flemings had thought they should invite him. He dreaded how different it would be yet for once he did not want to stay at home alone, he would resent that he had not gone, that he had taken the coward's way out and there was a part of him that longed to be friends with them still so, despite the negative feelings, he agreed, to Miss Piers' obvious surprise, to go.

By Saturday he had changed his mind and when he reached

the lovely house – fourteenth-century square stone, built for defence with a small tower and courtyard – he wished very much that he had stayed at home. The door was opened by a maid, the house was alight with candles and he could not help remembering Annabel's tiny kitchen and the child having gone to sleep in his arms.

In some ways he would be pleased to find Annabel more formal. He had been half in love with her ever since they had met and it was hard not to be bitter and envious of Ned, who apparently and with ease had everything. It was well known in the city that Ned's father had bought the house for them and even in the entrance there was expensive old furniture, the better to attest that Ned's background was coal-owner rich as his family had owned pits for two generations before him.

Divested of his coat, hat, scarf and gloves, Harry was escorted along the hall where a big fire blazed in a grey marble fireplace. Double doors were opened for him into a very big room and there several people were grouped around the fire, the men in evening dress, the women in gorgeous gowns.

Aidan Hedley was there with the woman he was about to marry, Lorna Carlyle, and to Harry's dismay Jason Taylor, his wife and his daughter. Mr Taylor came to him straight away and took him over to see his wife and daughter again and Harry was dumbfounded to discover that Elspeth Taylor smiled as though she was pleased to see him.

The double doors opened, a woman came in and Harry stared. It was Shona Rainbow. She was wearing a black dress, without doubt the cheapest dress in the room but the very severity and plainness of it made her stand out. She had no jewellery so that her wrists and neck were bare and her magnificent hair was swept up in the least complicated way it could be at the back and held with a black clip.

Her blue eyes had thick black lashes around them and she was thin, from grief he supposed. Her face was pale but it suited her. She looked around the room for a friend, her eyes faltered and Harry went over to her just as Ned reached them. He managed to greet Shona as though they were nothing but casual friends and Ned always diluted things and Harry was glad of it.

'Your house is magnificent,' Harry told Ned when the greetings were over.

'Isn't it?' Ned didn't sound totally pleased about his rise in the social world but Annabel seemed perfectly at home there, coming over to him and saying, 'Welcome to our humble new abode. Ned hates it.'

That made people laugh and several remarks were made about the little house in Sutton Street, how very small it had been, how inconvenient. Harry longed for it.

At dinner Harry was seated beside Elspeth Taylor and he was sorry that she was there. She should have been with a man her own age, fresh out of college, knee deep in books, clumsy and ardent. Harry cursed himself, especially when a woman seated opposite said archly, 'How lucky you are to have our eligible banker grace your home with his presence, Annabel. He never comes to any of my parties. I think he's afraid I'm going to find him a wife.' She looked directly at him and said, 'Don't you intend ever to marry, Mr Darling, and with such a name?'

Harry merely smiled in acknowledgement of the remark which he had heard so many times before that he had lost count.

'You have a lovely companion there.'

The 'lovely companion' blushed and turned away and Harry was furious with the stupid woman for making a young girl so embarrassed. Across the table he heard Caroline Atherton, a local barrister's wife, say past her husband to Shona, 'What line of business was your husband in, Mrs Rainbow?'

'He was a fisherman.'

'How interesting. Where was that?'

'Northumberland.'

'I would hate to live in such an out-of-the-way place. Did he have many people working for him?'

'He had his own boat.'

Mrs Atherton looked confused.

'It was a coble,' Shona said. 'Cod or lobster, you know, according to the season.'

'My wife is always telling me to eat more fish, good for the brain,' the woman's husband put in.

'Pity it didn't work, then,' Ned put in and made people laugh.

'It's all right for you, Ned, your father bought you this place. It's all very well you being a socialist but you're rich on the backs of miners.'

'Were you planning on staying for dessert, Felix, insulting me like that?' Ned said. 'You'll be very sorry if I throw you out. It's chocolate soufflé.'

When the little boy was brought downstairs to say goodnight he ignored his parents and stumbled across to Harry as though they were old friends. It was one of the most magical moments of Harry's life. The child's face lit and he held out both arms, no doubt to steady himself, and when he reached his goal he said something which very much resembled Harry's name.

'He likes attention since we had the new baby.' Annabel had recently given birth to their second child, a little girl, but for once Harry envied nobody. The child insisted on being pulled up on his knee, causing one woman to say, 'I didn't know you were good with children, Mr Darling.'

'Only ours,' Annabel said and Harry said nothing since it was the first time he had seen Thomas in months.

The nurse soon took away the child but Harry's evening was completely worthwhile now.

Later when the women were going off to drink tea Annabel came to him and said, 'We would like you to be godfather to Cicely.'

Harry stared at her.

'I'm not a religious person.'

'Oh, don't be so stuffy, nobody cares,' she said disarmingly. 'I shall take that as a yes and you will not dare to contradict me. And don't let Ned drink too much port,' she said as she left the room, 'he gets ruder as the evening goes on and the alcohol flows.'

Shona hated the way that the tea was brought in and the women talked of their children, she wished she could have stayed with the men and drunk port, she was sure she would like it. She felt safer there, men talked of innocuous things, sport and business and finance. Annabel however rescued her and talked to her about the shop and the newspapers she helped run and the magazine and her friends who were involved and she said, 'I shall introduce you to them, you'll like them all and you must come to the office and we'll go out for lunch. Come and look around the house, I'm dying to show it to you. You have taste so I know you'll like it.'

They left the room and in the dimness of the hall Annabel turned to her.

'I knew this was a mistake, I don't really want to be part of society here and God knows Ned doesn't. Of course Aidan and Lorna are all right but as for the rest of them, I thought I was doing Ned a favour but I don't think he cares. Come in here and tell me what you think of the colours.'

She opened the door which led into a pretty pink and raspberry coloured room where a fire burned.

'Ned's father chose it, Ned can't even choose a pair of socks.'

'I know nothing of such things but the colours are lovely,' Shona said. 'Who is the beautiful girl?'

'Oh, that's Elspeth Taylor. Her father and Harry seem very thick, wouldn't you say?'

'How awful for her, she's so very young.'

'Every woman in the place with an eligible daughter is considering these things even though Harry has no background. He doesn't hide the fact that he was once some orphan in the gutter. Elspeth seemed rather taken, didn't you think? Harry is gorgeous of course and more the gentleman than a good many men I could name but then Elspeth is so young and beautiful and unused and some men are addicted to such things.'

When they had walked around the rest of the house and Shona had admired everything they went back to drink tea with the others and then it was late and other people were leaving but Annabel said softly, 'I'll see people out and then Ned shall take you home.'

Having seen people beyond the doors Annabel came back with the information, 'Harry has said he will take you.'

Shona wanted to protest but couldn't.

And so it was that Harry saw her home and in his car. She hadn't been in a car before. It was big and strange and silver outside and smelled expensively of leather and cigars and made a lot of noise but she didn't want to talk to him anyway, she kept picturing him with that young girl and could not help being angry about how young the girl was and yet nobody would have thought anything about him marrying a girl that age, he was not exactly old.

She wanted to ask him about his life since she had left, what he had done, how long he had stayed with her father, who he had met, how he had become so very successful but she didn't know how to say it.

Harry stopped the car outside the shop. It was a wet dark night and the shop was in blackness.

Shona attempted to get out and Harry got out and helped her and then insisted on seeing her to the doors. Her fingers were so cold that she could barely unlock them. The icy air coming from inside made her move back slightly. Before he could speak she said, 'Thank you for bringing me home,' and she went inside and closed the doors.

Sixteen

Aidan Hedley hated Monday mornings, even though he worked at weekends, not so much since he and Lorna had planned their wedding, she objected to this and since she had a small child he wanted to be there with them but he had not quite broken himself of the habit, only sometimes he sat in his office on Mondays and dreamed of the house they were buying beside the river and how the three of them would be happy there.

This morning to make things worse he had an appointment with Jason Taylor. Aidan disliked Mr Taylor. He didn't know why, Jason had done nothing. He was a moderately successful businessman but his shop was the kind of place which intimidated ordinary people and would have been better suited to a big place like Newcastle or Sunderland.

Aidan's mother went there for her clothes. The idea made him shudder. His mother had been a beautiful woman once but she lived the lie that she had adored his father and once widowed had slipped into the kind of dull shapeless clothes which any woman of feeling would not have touched. No young men went there for their tailoring. No young women went there for their bridal gowns, they went to Newcastle. His sister Bea's friends did not dress themselves or their children at Taylor's store. It was left to the dull middle-aged middle-class people to shop there and those who didn't care what they looked like. Lorna said, and Lorna was very fashion-conscious, that Mr Taylor's wife and daughter would never have shopped in such a place.

Mr Taylor was punctual and Aidan said the right things, sat him down and listened and the more he listened the more alarmed he became because Mr Taylor said that he wanted Aidan to make an offer on his behalf to Shona Rainbow. Aidan had no idea what Shona would do but he wrote to her at the shop. He could have gone to see her but he didn't want to discuss this outside of his office. He made her an appointment for three days' time but said that he would see her whenever she chose if she let him know. He liked her and he had seen the way that she had so quickly learned to trust him. He could not betray her in any way.

She duly turned up at the appointed time on the Thursday morning and he told her what Mr Taylor had proposed and her mouth went into a line and she shook her head.

'It is a very good offer.'

'I don't want it.'

'You should consider it, even if only for a day or two. I know how serious he is about it, he's been planning for this ever since your father died, waiting for you to come back to see what you wanted to do.'

He stopped there because Shona was looking at him from glassy eyes which he knew meant unshed tears. She shook her head.

'I'm widowed, I have no child. The only future I have is to try for something else and the shop is that something else. It's the only way I can survive in a society such as this. I know you don't understand, how could you, but all money would do for me would be to give me a house and leisure and – what would I do?'

'I was obliged to put it to you because he asked me to. I'm not advising you to take it, I just wasn't sure whether the money would matter so much to you because you could do a great deal with it—'

'I feel in a way that I could fulfil my father's dreams. I know it's stupid but – tell Mr Taylor that I am grateful for his offer but I must decline it.'

'You're taking on a lot, you have no money, people here don't know you and you don't know what you're capable of yet. If this doesn't work out what will you do then? Take a few days to think about it, don't rush the decision,' Aidan said.

Shona was interested to see what Taylor's department store was like before she got very involved trying to do something similar. Having decided to turn down Jason Taylor's offer she then awoke in the night, going very warm at the idea of failure. Her father had failed and she had done nothing successful in her life so far, she turned over as this idea hit her and then turned on to her back and stared up into the cold darkness. She thought of the money, she thought of how she could have got away from there, gone to a completely new town where nobody was aware of her circumstances and become somebody new, somebody else.

She had argued politely with her solicitor – she liked to think of Aidan Hedley as hers personally somehow, it made her feel an importance she lacked in everything else she did – but Aidan had insisted on her going back to think about it and now she was glad he had insisted on not giving a reply to Jason Taylor straight away. She went back to sleep having told herself that she would go and see Mr Hedley first thing in the morning and take the money and take a train away from here.

She fell asleep instantly, comforted that she had changed her mind but when the morning arrived, even though the shop was freezing, she changed her mind again and began looking forward to the day and the things that she might possibly achieve and she knew that she could not run away from this because if she didn't try to make it work what else would she do with her life that would matter? And also she had other people to consider now.

While she was sitting over her first cup of tea in the kitchen with Gino she decided that she would get ready and go over and take a proper look at Taylor's shop and see if it was the kind of thing she was trying to do. That should make her decision easier, if his place was so good that there was no room for competition she would take the money and start up somewhere else.

The store was not far, you could almost see it from her windows, it was on the edge of the Market Place and Silver Street, a big building that took up most of the space with tiny shops at either side.

Mr Taylor sold everything, she thought. The outside of the building was much more impressive than her own, black and gold with one of those men standing outside, all dressed up to see people safely through the doors. She thought it looked very classy and her heart went down.

She nodded hello to him as he opened the door. Inside all

was dark and gloomy. Her footsteps were dulled by thick carpet and she gazed around. This place would have been better placed on one of the big Newcastle streets, like Northumberland Street. It was hushed. She could see several assistants, all of them dressed in black, and Shona thought it was obvious that nobody was having any fun here.

A woman came over and Shona had the impression that she knew exactly how cheap Shona's clothes were. She had never had time to look for good clothes and somehow never wanted them, she was quite happy with the market or a little shop in Alnwick, it had seemed so wasteful to spend on such things when James was coming home soaked and frozen from hauling nets through his red hands and almost sick because the sea had been mountainous that day. You could never tell what was going to happen.

She looked Shona up and down.

'Can I help madam with anything?'

'Do you have a cafe?'

The woman looked astonished.

'No.'

'A toy department?'

The woman hesitated.

'We have a children's clothing department on the top floor.'

How inconvenient, Shona thought, to make mothers drag children up two flights of stairs.

'And the men's clothing department?'

'Tailoring is at the back of the store on this floor.'

There again, Shona thought, a mistake. Men didn't like shopping as far as she knew and to have to walk into the depths of such a place would put the majority of them off. Not that it would have helped if tailoring had been upstairs, it would have made things worse.

There was a perfume counter in the centre of the floor and she would have put it nearer the door had the smells been attractive but the air was heavy with musk and everything was under the counter so the shine of the bottles and pretty design could not reflect through the lighting or what daylight was coming inside and entice women to purchase the bottles which would look so pretty on their dressing tables.

The women's clothing was upstairs, she thought they were in dowdy colours, beige, brown, sludge green, navy blue, the only shine being gold buttons with navy blue jackets and spotted scarves.

There was an extensive fur department and here she could not fault Mr Taylor, if you wanted furs this was the place to come and several women were looking and one woman was trying on what looked to Shona like mink but she wasn't sure having never seen mink before. It was a strange colour, almost like sand, and full length.

The woman was small and it overpowered her but the assistant was telling her as she gazed into the mirror how beautiful it was on her, no doubt because it would be so very expensive. It would have taken a tall slender woman to carry off the coat, anybody with any shape would have looked like a dumpling in it.

A fur department, Shona decided, needed a huge investment of money to carry racks of such things but she went over and touched the coat she would have liked herself. It was beaver lamb, warm to the touch and had velvet pockets.

'Would madam like to try on the coat?' enquired a voice behind her.

She turned to the assistant smiling her thanks.

'Oh thank you,' she said, 'but I couldn't possibly afford it.'

The woman said nothing and moved away but it occurred to Shona at that moment – not for things like the beaver lamb, that would be too much of an indulgence for almost everyone she knew, except Annabel Fleming probably, but she thought that if she opened her shop she could use the method of payment which many people carried on with their butcher or their greengrocer where they had an account and paid at the end of the month but they could pay off the price of bigger things at so much a fortnight or monthly, being careful of course of the people involved in such a scheme but if people did not have a winter coat and could have the garment at the beginning of the winter and pay for it over the winter and it was something which would last them several years she thought this a good idea.

The shoe department was a surprise, the shoes had little

ornamentation and were made for comfort rather than frivolity and she did not quite understand why she was disappointed. Women needed serviceable shoes but then they also needed shoes for dancing and shoes for parties and shoes to look down on and be glad of when the minister's sermon went on a little long.

She brought to mind the Hans Christian Andersen story of the Red Shoes and the girl who begged the woodsman to chop off her feet because she had been condemned to dance for ever because she wore her dancing shoes to church. Women should have more dancing shoes and more opportunities to wear pretty things even if they were poor. Church shoes could not be worn for dancing even around the kitchen with a baby or a broom.

She thought that women even needed shoes that they might keep because they had once been young and danced through the night in impossible high heels. Shona thought at this point that she was getting carried away. She went into the food department at the back of the store. It had clean tiled floors and a good smell of coffee but of course no cafe and the food was expensive, luxuries, the kind of thing which even rich people kept for Christmas, peaches in brandy, chocolate almonds tied up in pretty ribbon.

It would soon be Christmas, she tried not to think about it, she thought back to the Christmases in the village with James and thought how lonely they had been because none of his family had anything to do with them but then her Christmases with her father when she was small had been just as bad, he spent most of the time in the pubs and Christmas Day in bed sleeping it off.

In fact the only Christmases she had enjoyed were the ones after Harry had arrived. They would buy special food and sit over the fire instead of going to a market, they would sleep in late that day and if it was not pouring with rain they would walk around the river in the afternoon.

She brushed the thoughts from her mind and recalled the evening party at Annabel's house and how he had barely spoken to her. What did you have to say to someone after fifteen years? She hardly recognized him, so quiet, so withdrawn. She went back to thinking of how this store should have had some kind of place like a cafe so that people could meet their friends, it would have been a focus. As it was there was hardly anybody at all among the lovely confectionery and fruits.

It could have been argued that since the Silver Street cafe was nearby there was no need. There were plenty of traditional cakes to buy, the biscuits were plain and there was nothing to attract children. She went upstairs to the furniture department. It was all well made in heavy dark wood but very expensive and the buyer would have needed large rooms to house it.

She lingered over the curtains, remembering the days when she had sold such items on the market not far from here. Once again she was asked if she needed anything and when she said that she was just looking was asked 'whether madam had a large house which needed curtaining'. Shona replied that madam didn't have a house at all but thanked her for the help.

The thing that mattered most, she thought, as she left was that the whole shop was practically empty. Working-class people would not favour such a shop, could not afford much, it catered exclusively for people who had money. Other folk would be intimidated and she had the feeling that a great many people, wanting more variety than there was here, would take a train into Newcastle where the shops glittered and enticed.

She went to Aidan before she could change her mind again, stopped halfway there even though she had an appointment and then went on. She did want the shop, she knew there would be difficulties but she wanted to be here. This was her home, she would not leave it now to go somewhere else – there was nowhere else she wanted to go, she would stay here and make this work.

She was surprised, two days later, to find a middle-aged man wearing a very expensive suit framed in the doorway of her store. She recognized him as Jason Taylor, they had met at Ned and Annabel's dinner party. She had heard a noise and come forward from within the depths where she was trying to put together ideas for opening at least the rest of the floor at some time soon, she was clearing out and talking to a joiner Ned had found for her about the various shelving she would need, she wanted a men's clothing department further along beside two big windows, she was even thinking that there would be a separate entrance so that men could be enticed into the shop and she wanted to sell alongside the clothing things like cigars and bottles of spirits, books on relevant subjects like sport and shooting and fishing and she wanted to sell clothing for spring after Christmas was well over.

She also wanted a women's clothing department there, again with a separate entrance to the side so that it was within reach of the cafe she was planning to extend – it was nothing much at the moment but people already counted it as theirs and many of them arrived daily, they seemed not to mind that the shop was a progressive enterprise and that parts of it were not yet open or completed. They liked the ongoingness and that they were part of it, she thought she was not just building a store here, she was building a meeting place in the centre of the small city which everyone would know and hopefully want to come to.

She came forward to the main doors, leaving the joiner measuring the walls where they would be placing men's shirts and sweaters. She couldn't think what he was doing there. He wasn't smiling so she didn't think it was a friendly visit and he said in a booming voice, 'I understand you've been into my shop. I thought I might repay the visit.'

'Certainly. Can I give you coffee?'

He gazed around him and said, 'It's a very strange-looking shop.'

'I intend it to be quite different from anything that has been done before.'

'I don't think a city this size needs another big shop. I have made you a very good offer for the premises through my solicitor, I'm interested to know why you have decided so very quickly that you won't take up my very generous offer.'

'This was my father's dream,' she said before she could think.

'I knew him vaguely. I don't think he would ever have made it come true. He had so little talent for this kind of work.'

'Can I show you around?'

She did so, rather nervously, she wasn't sure what he was doing here and he said little other than that he thought it was very ambitious. He asked her about her life in Northumberland and she tried not to say much about it other than that she had lived near Alnwick. Mr Taylor stayed for about an hour. When he left Shona found that she was very warm in spite of the fact that only part of the downstairs of her shop was heated at the moment and she stood outside for a little while, trying to cool down and not give any thought to him or his all-seeing gaze.

Shona travelled to Darlington and Newcastle to see what other department stores were like and she didn't think much of their reserve. They were not interesting or exciting, the fashions were old, a lot of the stock seemed completely out of date, or so Annabel said when she went with her.

Shona could see too that they were not catering for the people around them – everything was expensive and that would put off the people who were less well off, also they had pompous men on every floor, supposedly to direct people to where they were going but they were so dressed up that Shona would have had difficulty in asking them anything and she did not think a good many other people would have managed it either.

The furniture departments were dull and dark, the cafes she saw had no interesting cakes or menus and only old women frequented them and that she thought was because they had little choice and some leisure. The chairs and tables were neither bright nor attractive. Shona and Annabel walked along High Row, the main street in Darlington, and there Shona saw a good women's wear shop with bright fashionable clothes, reasonably priced and other more serviceable wear for everyday, and she went forward as the shop keeper came to her and she said, 'I am opening a department store in Durham City and I wondered if we could open a branch of your shop within mine.' She told the woman her name and the woman, a little older than she was, Miss Everton, smiled and shook her hand and all three sat down together and discussed it and agreed that she would come through the following week and see whether it was a good idea. They talked about the place within the department store where the women's clothing could operate and agreed that she would come the following Tuesday. She worked with her sister and her sister would come with her.

Shona did the same at the best tailor's in town and received the same response, Mr Barnes would come through to Durham the same day and they would have a meeting and he thought this was a very good idea, he had wanted to expand but wasn't sure whether he could go about it, since he could not afford to rent another shop, but he had a member of staff who was interested and might move there on his behalf, should it prove a possibility.

She and Annabel practically danced back to the station, they were so excited at the prospect.

On the way home Annabel leaned across to her when they were on the train and said, 'You are coming to Cicely's christening. Aidan's sister, Bea, is to be godmother to Cicely. It would be a good opportunity for you to meet her. Ned is publishing her latest work next week, we could have a book signing at the front of your shop.'

'But, Annabel, it's nowhere near finished.'

'It doesn't matter. People are curious. We could find somebody to play carols on that old piano you bought and you and I and Thomas could spend tomorrow putting up a tree, I've got lots of ornaments, my mother would help us, she's very good at organizing things and she and my stepfather are coming to stay for Christmas.'

'I could keep the store open late and Susan might provide food and drink, she's been marvellous with the cafe. I just wish I had something more to offer people at this point.'

'We could open the doors to people, in the evening. Have a grand opening just for the front of the shop, it would be a start.'

Seventeen

It was difficult to ignore Harry, Shona thought, and she wanted to. On the day of the christening she watched him running about on Palace Green with Annabel's little boy before the service began in the cathedral in the cold morning.

It was the first light-hearted thing she had seen him do, the little boy running away so that Harry would run after him, and then shrieking and giggling when he was caught. Harry held the child up high against the sunlight and there was a peculiar pang in Shona's breast which told her that she should have been part of something similar, yet she could not and stood, disconsolate for a few moments.

Annabel had not stinted on her invitations to her child's christening party and these included Jason Taylor, his wife and daughter and Shona could not help but notice that Elspeth Taylor left her parents talking and went to Harry, putting her hand through his arm in what Shona thought was a particularly intimate way, as though they knew one another very well, causing him to turn and excuse himself from the people he was with to find her smiling up at him in a way that Shona had not realized she would resent.

She did realize it within seconds and thought what a horrible response it was. Harry was nothing to do with her, if he had chosen a bride then so he ought, she thought it would be good for him. He had never meant to her nearly as much as James had and he never would.

After the ceremony they all went off to Annabel and Ned's house, Bea Hedley with Cicely safely in her arms and Thomas not letting go of Harry's hand and gazing at him from time to time as though he feared Harry might disappear in a puff of smoke.

When Annabel had made sure everybody had enough to eat and drink she brought Shona a glass of wine and said, 'I think Harry is very popular, neither Elspeth Taylor nor my little boy has left his side all day. He must have proposed to her. Have you heard anything?'

Shona shook her head and took the glass of wine and sipped it. Elspeth Taylor's gloved hands were fastened around Harry's arm and it was definitely a possessive gesture. She was envious of anybody's happiness, she thought with disgust, and moved away. Ned came to her shortly afterwards.

'I hear tell that you might be persuaded to sell your shop. Is this true?'

'Where did you hear it?'

'I'm a newspaper man, I hear everything, but I didn't believe it though by all accounts Jason Taylor has offered a considerable sum. You probably don't need my advice—' He stopped there.

'I would value it, even though my decision is made and he knows it.'

'It wouldn't be any fun if you sold.'

That made Shona laugh and she was glad that he had spoken in such a way.

'His own store is so horrible that Annabel won't set foot inside it. She says the fashions are years old.'

Shona, glad of somebody to talk to, told him about her visit to Taylor's though she was sure that Annabel had already recounted what she told but he listened and nodded and he said, 'You could take him on and better him even though he has had a huge bank loan to finance him.'

'Has he?'

Ned looked surprised.

'I thought you would know, everybody else does. Darling's Bank loaned him a fortune. It's common knowledge that Taylor is in debt, I didn't think anybody would loan him the money, least of all Harry, being so shrewd. He may not get it back. I dare say when Jason Taylor realized you wouldn't sell he had a dozen other places for it to go.'

'Why would Harry do that?'

'He plays deep.'

She felt certain this was some kind of gaming term and it made her feel uncomfortable. All that afternoon she avoided even looking at Harry. He must have his reasons for such things and if he thought she wanted to sell then there was no point in him not loaning the money because if she did sell – but no, he must have known surely that she would not. She remembered Ned's words, that Jason Taylor desperately needed the money and at the end of the day she went to Ned and very quietly asked him if Jason Taylor was not making money and had debts then what would he use as insurance against the loan.

'He has nothing but his house as far as I know.'

'So if he cannot pay what he owes with interest within a certain amount of time Harry gets the house.'

'It is a very handsome house.'

'And do you think Harry wants it?'

'I don't know. I suppose if he'd wanted a house by now he could long since have bought one. He doesn't need to come by it that way.'

And that, Shona thought, was the problem. What on earth did Harry want with such a house, and if Harry was planning to marry Elspeth Taylor he would hardly be putting her parents out of their home? Ned saw her looking across to where Elspeth Taylor was laughing at something Harry had said.

'He won't marry her.'

'Why not?'

'Why would he? There are lots of young women who need to marry somebody with money, why would he want her?'

'She's very beautiful.'

Ned was watching Shona closely, she tried not to be aware of it.

'You were friends, weren't you? Harry doesn't have many friends, I think Annabel and I are about the only people he sees and even then he doesn't offer invitations, he just waits for them.'

Elspeth Taylor was indeed beautiful but Harry was not moved by her. He had been surprised at how she had come to him, so openly as though she wanted people to think they were very good friends. He had realized by now that her father was desperate enough to do anything, even to encourage his daughter so that Harry might fall in love with her. How little he knows me, Harry thought. She was to him like any other beautiful girl who had been thrust at him, the only difference was that she had sufficient confidence not to agree with everything he said but then he did not find her interesting.

How could she be, she was eighteen, she had not lived, she knew nothing but what her parents had allowed her to know and like so many well-bred young women her knowledge was only of books and gardens and boring afternoons in her mother's sitting room and clothes and social events. She was not witty or outlandish, she was not any of the things that might have endeared her to him, but then no woman ever was. Best of his acquaintance he liked Annabel Fleming, but Annabel had come from top London society and it showed.

He would have married her had he been given the chance but then it was not real love, just a mixture of lust and frivolity, she made him laugh. He had only ever loved Shona and he had not fallen in love as people said they did, it was part gratitude for food and warmth and her saving of his life, no little thing but it was to do with day to day, talk and food and the market and the people and her father and all her concerns and even the horse, he thought, old Julius.

He remembered how she had stroked the horse's nose and talked to him, walked through the streets with him to the Three Tuns, he had such good memories of their times together when they were young. They both talked to Julius, they had history, they had no present and he thought, no future.

There was nothing quite as damping to one's affections as knowing that another man had claimed the woman who mattered and even now he could see that she was still very much in love with James Rainbow and why should she not be, he dared say their life in Northumberland had been sweet even though there was no child. Her grief was such that the loss must be enormous and no earthly man could compete with that.

And he didn't want to, that was the relief of it, he was content that she should be there, he had nothing against her. He was almost happy to let Elspeth prattle on, it saved him from other people's conversation, from their questions and their curious eyes, they always wanted to know more about him.

He couldn't see why, he was hardly fascinating and yes, he had made money from nothing but so what? They thought he had things to hide and there was nothing, no social life, no women, he did not gamble and drink and go to whores. All he did was work and there was no conversation in that except to other bankers.

Eventually, from sheer boredom, he turned to Elspeth and said, 'What are you doing here? Don't you have a nice young man somewhere?'

He was startled by her response, by her quick denial, that there was nobody, that she could never think of anybody beyond—

'Oh, come on,' Harry said, 'there must be somebody.'

The tears filled her eyes. She shook her head violently. Harry put her hand through his arm and walked her away from everyone else and he said, 'You can't marry a man for a house.'

She understood him, he could see.

'Or because your father thinks it a good idea.'

'Most girls do,' she said.

'I'm sure they do. I'm not sure it's always a success.'

'Dragon's Field is very important to us.'

'It's only a building.' It was such a lie, he almost wished he hadn't said it but he meant that to her it was only a house, or it should be.

'It's our family home.'

'Other people owned it before you and others will afterwards. You shouldn't give your freedom or your future for it.'

She said nothing.

'If I can help I will.'

Elspeth shook her head.

'There's nobody else here. I won't tell,' Harry said softly.

She considered and then she looked up and she said, 'William Cook.'

This was easy. Harry was delighted with the simplicity of it and could have laughed. He knew himself so well, he could sort this out, make it work. William Cook worked for Harry, was a bright young man from a steady if unremarkable background, his father was a schoolmaster, they lived in Hallgarth Street and Harry had been considering whether he should promote William, who had a fine mind.

'William is about to become manager of the Bishop Auckland branch, if he so chooses, and there is a good house to go with it and since bank managers are very often married don't you think that this might work?'

She went on staring at him for some moments and then she said, 'Do you really mean it?'

'Certainly, I do.'

'Oh, but I can't let my parents down.'

'Elspeth, I like you very much but don't you think I'm a bit old for you?'

'It's only about fifteen years.'

'Exactly and – I do admire how beautiful you are but I'm not going to propose marriage to you.'

'You have to,' she said bleakly.

'I will help you and William to marry.'

He talked like this to her until all traces of the tears had gone and then she turned to him.

'Oh, thank you so much, Mr Darling. You have no idea what you have done.'

Harry had never felt quite so old. He did not like to point out to her that she would have a battle to fight and only if she and William Cook really cared for one another would they get through that battle and be married but a promotion and a house for William were a good start.

'There is a rumour that you loaned Jason Taylor money to buy my shop.'

Harry looked taken aback, as if he thought Shona might be speaking to someone else and then he recovered.

She had been about to leave, the celebrations were over but her conversation with Ned played on her mind and she didn't know why but it made her unhappy.

'I can't talk about that,' he said but she could tell by his eyes that something was wrong, her instincts had been correct.

'Really?' She was looking at him very straight now and not pleased with his closed expression. 'I come into the category of business, do I? But you know me well enough to assume that I wouldn't sell.'

'We haven't met in fifteen years until very recently and your financial circumstances can't be easy especially with starting the shop. Besides, he came to me months ago just after your father died, it was nothing to do with you.'

'Is it something to do with Elspeth Taylor?'

Harry didn't say anything.

'What is Dragon's Field like?'

'I've never been there.'

She might not have seen him for fifteen years but she could tell when he was lying and there was something else, a distance about him which had got bigger and bigger over those years, his manner was dismissive of other people at best.

'Harry—'

'Can I take you back to the shop? I have to pass it on my way home.'

'It's a hotel,' she pointed out.

Harry looked gravely at her.

'I had noticed,' he said.

Eighteen

The church which Shona usually attended was the one in the Market Place, simply because it was the nearest to her, but the Sunday she went next she found that she was listening carefully to the organ being played and she stayed well past the end of the service since the old man seemed happy to go on playing. When he was finally finished there was only the two of them left and he smiled and came over.

'You're the lady who is opening the big shop. I used to play in music shops, you know, it helped to sell the pianos.'

'You play beautifully,' Shona said.

'It's my whole life since my wife died. We have no children. I look around at other people's families and . . .' He didn't go on but Shona knew exactly what he meant, she did that herself. That was when she had the idea.

'Mr Simpson, would there be any chance you might come across to the shop sometimes and play in the cafe? You probably think that's beneath you.'

Mr Simpson assured her it was not so and his enthusiasm was catching so in the end she led him across the road and introduced him to the piano. She had just had it tuned and he said it was quite a good instrument and demonstrated this by sitting down and playing several of her favourite pieces and when she told him she couldn't pay him much his face brightened and he said he would be glad to be there, he hadn't much to do during the day any more and he would be pleased with the money.

The day of the book launch the shop was decorated with a big tree which was to be lit with candles and there would be a carol service and Mr Simpson would play all the carols and there would be tea and coffee and hot chocolate which Gino had made and mince pies which had been made at the Silver Street cafe.

They had paper chains across the ceilings in the various departments. All the fires were lit so that the place was warm, the music floated up and around through the shop, and people came, so many of them that Shona was amazed, and when their voices lifted in all her favourite carols she was glad. The smell of chocolate and mince pies filled the front of the shop and she gave out simple toys to the children – it was a small expense and their parents were so grateful. Annabel and Ned had donated Christmas cakes and Aidan Hedley had paid for hats and scarves and mittens to be given to the children as presents. His staff also came.

The real coup of the evening was that Gino spent a great deal of time making chocolate stars so that every child who came could have one.

From that evening forward the shop was not just a place for people to buy but a place for them to come. They didn't have to have money, they could sit in the book department and borrow books if they liked though the richer people bought and in quantity since Shona wrapped each parcel in red and green chiffon. Mr Simpson played Christmas songs and women sat in newly painted yellow chairs and ate Christmas cake which had been made at the Silver Street cafe.

The Silver Street cafe had such a reputation that it could afford to keep itself and Mrs Rainbow's Emporium going in food. Food could be taken away, whole meals if anybody should want them – and a good many people did, snacks and cakes and breakfast rolls and the boxes and bags for them had the Silver Street cafe written on them in silver, courtesy of Ned with silver paint and stencils and the ordinary bags for other items had Mrs Rainbow's Emporium written below a rainbow.

When each working day was over after this and she was busy Shona would retreat upstairs and there she had her new family, all the people she had taken in who were working for her. There was a kitchen and a bathroom and each person had their own big room and in it a decent bed and somewhere to put their clothes. It took time, Shona acknowledged, but when she made more money she would make things better for the employees.

As it was all the employees loved it, she could see. Mr

Simpson had moved in when Shona discovered his damp house up beyond Old Elvet. They liked one another's company or if they didn't they could go away to their own rooms and have privacy. They all loved Gino and he would sing in Italian, he would sing opera and Mr Simpson would play the piano. It didn't always work but it was always fun.

Shona made an office for herself down the side of the building. It was a very small room, she had no idea what it had been used for prior to this but she felt as though she needed a place to herself so that she could think. There was a pretty black fireplace in there with green and pink tiles and it had for some stupid reason a tiny patch of ground outside surrounded by a wall which was high enough to keep out anybody's gaze or anybody's person.

Inside it a door led into the tiny grass patch so that if there was ever enough sun you could sit outside or the day was fine you could at least open the door and there was an old stone bird-bath and the blackbirds would spend time showering their wings and tossing their heads and there were long-neglected bushes at the sides and from here various small birds alighted on to the lawn, blue tits and long-tailed tits in grey and black and a robin who obviously thought he owned the area and looked boldly at Shona so that when she threw out nuts and seeds which she had stolen from her own kitchen the robin would come close and cock his head as though he was listening to what she was saying and he would come right up to her.

There were thrushes too and pigeons who strutted about picking up whatever fell to the grass and sometimes the air was black with rooks and if the weather was bad she could see the gulls circling and crying and it reminded her of home so much that it blurred her vision. She could picture the life she had had and thought never to lose, she had not believed that nothing was for ever, she had been happy. Now she was busy, that was the best she could manage.

It was completely private there for the first few weeks but it didn't last as people were always wanting to know where she was to ask her something but sometimes she could slip in there unnoticed and spend a little time to herself.

* * *

As the weather grew worse through January and February into March the streets were full of people who were cold and could not afford the price of a cup of coffee and they would hang around in the shop, pretending they wanted to buy goods, sometimes they stole small items, nothing valuable, because Shona didn't sell anything valuable that was on show and she would watch them and let them get away with it. She was not, she thought, the most practical of shopkeepers.

Often she went out and offered them jobs, cleaning up inside the front door, or dropping through letterboxes the leaflets which Ned Fleming had printed. She invited everyone to the special times the shop had, to view new clothes, to see the latest styles, and she knew they came for the food and Ned soon realized what she was doing and he would contribute, he had made hundreds of sandwiches and tea was cheap to make so there were always tea urns on the go and he would leave copies of his newspapers everywhere and Annabel would bring great boxes of biscuits and they would have a band to play to make the whole thing so festive, so important, and during the cold nights Shona would not turn people from her doors. Ned and Annabel had bought up a big hall across the market square and opened it and gave hungry people bread and soup and a safe place to stay. They slept on the floor or on makeshift beds.

Shona did not forget about her conversation with Harry about Jason Taylor's house and she was so intrigued that she went to see Dragon's Field. She thought it was a very strange name for a place and when she asked about it everybody seemed to have heard of it. It lay outside of the city and the day she chose was fine and bright and there was a covering of snow so she walked, enjoying the way that the sun came out and made the snow glisten. She thought about her shop and how things were moving forward and she was glad of it.

It was indeed a very handsome Georgian house, ivy covered the front of it and long square-paned windows matched evenly on either side. She did not want to trespass, it would have been rude, so she kept beyond the gates and as she did so a carriage rolled up and to her dismay it stopped and Mrs Taylor whom she knew slightly by now put her head out and said, 'Why, Mrs Rainbow, I thought it was you. Do climb in and come and have tea with me.'

Shona had never been so embarrassed. She didn't like Jason Taylor, she was determined not to like his wife but Mrs Taylor was all smiles, complimented her on her shop, said she liked the fashions and styles of the new women's department store and had had coffee in Mrs Rainbow's Emporium that very morning.

'But my husband mustn't know. He would think it traitorous.'

They reached the front door, they went up the steps and there were stone likenesses of dragons which Shona didn't like somehow, they didn't seem to go with the house, and she went inside and for Shona it was almost like fainting. She had to grab on to the door, she didn't know why.

Mrs Taylor didn't notice and went on chattering as they reached the hall and then a maid came forward and she asked for tea to be sent to the drawing room and she talked on about how the chapel had been added and how they had always intended to have dances in the ballroom. The hallway itself was not dark so Shona had no idea why her mood came down and down into blackness.

She shook it off, she thought she must be coming down with flu or something. Divested of her outdoor things she followed her hostess into an enormous room and there she had a terrible pain right across her forehead so that even Mrs Taylor noticed how pale she had become and made her sit down.

'My dear,' she said, 'have you been working too hard? Do sit there and when the tea comes you shall have some straight away.'

The pain receded, the blackness went, Shona could not understand herself, it was ridiculous. The snow beyond the windows made the gardens look like a fairy tale, the steps led down to bare black trees at some distance away and the fires, two of them, burned merrily. Mrs Taylor talked of spring saying how much she disliked the cold weather and Shona listened to her chatter and glanced uneasily around the room.

It was lovely, there were delicate ornaments of Georgian figures wearing pale colours, paintings of hunting scenes, a cabinet full of some kind of china, gold and pink, and thick rugs upon the floor. The room was charming, friendly, just like the woman who was mistress of it. Every minute got longer and longer until Shona could have sworn she had been there a week. She made herself drink the tea and then said she must get back, she had work to do, she had just fancied a walk, the day was so pretty. Mrs Taylor tried to send for the carriage to take her but Shona insisted on walking back.

Once she was back beyond the gates Shona was well again but looked back at the place and shuddered. She did not understand it. She was exhausted, went to bed early, expecting that the next day she would be worse but after a night's sleep she was full of energy and could not imagine what had happened to her.

Harry was more and more haunted by the idea that he would end up owning Dragon's Field. He couldn't sleep because of what he had done and cursed Jason Taylor in the cold dark hours of the nights. He went over and over what Jason Taylor had said to him and tried to convince himself that the man was a liar as well as all the other faults he had. Harry determined to do nothing about it but in the end he went to see Aidan.

Aidan was clearly astonished both because Harry had made the appointment at such short notice and also because Harry never came to him. It was an unspoken agreement that Aidan always went to the bank. Aidan said nothing as Harry marched into his office, waving away offers to take his coat, and slumped down into a chair, head low.

Harry sat there for a few moments and then looked straight at his solicitor's puzzled face.

'I've got a problem.'

Aidan looked further mystified. Harry smiled to himself. Aidan would think that he had done something he shouldn't have, got a girl pregnant and had to buy her off, or – Harry couldn't think and watched Aidan's face go into a nice blank line.

'Whatever it is—' he said.

'Would you?'

'Why, yes.'

'No matter what it was?'

The mask came off.

'Anything.'

'You shouldn't ever say that, Aidan, but I won't forget it, thanks.'

In the silence Aidan waited.

'The thing is I want some information but I don't want to go about it myself, at least not to begin with.' He hesitated.

'Tell me, then.'

'There was a woman—' Aidan's back went rigid, Harry could see it and he shook his head. 'Not like that. She worked for the St Clair family. You have heard of them.'

'Of course.'

'A long time ago. She was called Ida Morrison, she was the cook.'

'How long ago are we talking here?'

'About twenty-five years. She could be dead.'

'You want her found? You don't have an address, then?'

'I think she had family locally but – she lived in so maybe not.'

'How old was she then?'

'I don't know. And there's something else too. Did your firm deal with the buying of the St Clair house?'

'Possibly. I could find out. We keep records of everything. It would have been my father or Mr Jameson.'

'I need you to do this yourself. I don't want anybody to know and then I want you to give me an address for her and if you could find out the details of the house sale.'

'Do you mean how much?'

'No, I mean why was it sold and how and who profited.'

'I see.'

Mrs Morrison was not easy to find, Aidan discovered. She had married again. He wished people wouldn't, it made his job so much harder. And she had moved. He ended up in the back streets of Esh Winning, a big mining village a few miles out of the city. There dirty children threw stones at him and when he turned and shouted they ran away. He had tried the front door but nobody had answered and he was aware that many people always used the back door so he went around to the back, counted the houses until he reached what he thought was the correct one and went up the yard. Eventually the door was opened by an elderly woman.

'Is there a Mrs Baker living in this row?'

She looked him up and down.

'I'm not her.'

'No, I know, I need to contact her.'

'Aye, she lives at number five, just along.' The woman pointed.

Aidan went off without explaining himself as he could not and the woman gazed after him. Later that day he sent Harry a handwritten note.

In the early evening Harry drove out of Durham. He left the car at some distance from the village and walked. He met no one, it was very cold, the streets were empty. He found the right place with little difficulty but unlike Aidan he went to the front of the row and banged on the door of the house where Aidan had thought Mrs Morrison now Baker lived and when a woman came to the door he had asked if she had been Mrs Morrison and he had made up a story, he told her that his mother had been a housemaid and had worked for the St Clairs and the family had lost touch and he was hoping that she might be able to help. He told her that his name was Harold Darling and she smiled and invited him in and said what a strange and rather nice name.

Inside all was neat and tidy and a brave fire burned in the kitchen. There was no fire in the front room, she said, except on Sundays though she would have lit it had she known she would have a visitor. He asked when she had worked at the house and she said she had left when old Mr St Clair died.

'Not a nice man,' she said. 'So what was the woman's name?'

'Elsie Wilson.'

'I don't remember her. Mind you, people came and went, they never stayed. There was never any wages.'

They settled down by the fire and she offered him tea which

Harry refused. He didn't want to waste time. He didn't want to be there. Half a dozen times that day he had tried to persuade himself not to go. What good would it do? But his mind was not easy and he kept remembering Jason Taylor's face and the sincerity with which he spoke about Dragon's Field.

'Why?' was all Harry said and she said, 'Oh, the old man he had no money.'

'Had he done something with it?'

'I don't really know, I don't think there'd been any money for a long time and gradually the good furniture went and then the pictures and the horses from the stables and the animals from the fields and it was a shame to see it. Looks like going the same way again, so I hear. Very proud Mrs Taylor is, nowt's good enough for a woman who's had nowt.'

'I thought she came from a good family.'

'Good they might have been in the sense that they were very proud and pride's a sin but they had no money and she has to have everything apparently, jewels and furs and so on, and that daughter of theirs, she's the same. He was besotted with her, you see. He didn't have the money either but some folk do nothing but spend.'

'Do you remember him buying the place?'

'Oh aye, I walked out when the old man died, hadn't been paid in months. Dreadful it was but then you would know. Was she a relative?'

'My aunt, we think, but we've lost touch.'

'I was glad to get out. Nothing good ever happened at that place. The old man dropped dead. Good way to go.'

'What about his son?'

She looked perplexed.

'He didn't have a son. He was the last of them, the last of the St Clairs. Good riddance to them, I say.'

'I thought there were children, grandchildren.'

She shook her head.

'I heard it said the son and his – his wife ran away and left a child there.'

'I think you're mixing it up. Maybe your Elsie was fond of telling stories. There was nobody.'

'She said there was a boy—'

'Oh, him. Oh, he was nothing to do with the family, he was company for the old man, I couldn't see what the old feller saw in him, scraggy looking little lad.'

'He wasn't a St Clair?'

'Just the opposite.' She laughed a little. 'Some lass gave birth in a hedgeback and we got lumbered.'

Harry couldn't speak.

'Found him, the old man did, like a stray dog. He would take things in. Most of them we got shot of but the bairn, he would have him there. Mind you there were never any visitors, nobody ever came to the house, and I think he taught the lad to read so when his eyes began to go the lad would read to him. It was his only pleasure, I think. When was Elsie there, if you remind me I might remember, you know?'

Harry mentioned a year at random and she laughed and said that was before she had been at the house so she didn't think she could help and he tried to ask casually about the girl who had the child but she only said that nobody knew anything about her, she had gone off leaving the child and that was all.

Harry didn't remember walking back to the car or driving back to Durham and all he could think was of hearing or reading somewhere that sometimes it was better not to dig things up, not to go back, that it was sometimes better not to know. He wished he had thought of it sooner and then knew that nothing would have stopped him, that Jason Taylor coming to him in the first place and talking of Dragon's Field and all his young life brought it to the front of his mind in such a way he could not help himself, he was trying to make sense of any of it, just a little but none of it seemed so now.

The next day he went to work as usual and mid-morning Aidan Hedley came in with news about the sale of Dragon's Field and Mrs Baker had been right and Jason Taylor had told the truth. There was no heir, the man he had thought his grandfather had had no children, the St Clair family line had died out. The house was run down then, the land had almost all been sold off, there was nothing of value left, it was in very bad repair.

'I want to call in the loan,' Harry said. 'How soon can I do that?'

'The document which I drew up says that you can demand the money back at any time, the interest varying of course depending on how long it is and since it has been a short time then it wouldn't benefit you financially to call it in now. It may benefit you in other ways of course. The house would be yours in a matter of weeks.' He paused and when the silence had gone on for what felt to Harry like a long time though he would have let it fill the room indefinitely Aidan said, 'That's what you want me to do?'

'Yes.'

'And when he can't pay?'

'Evict him.'

Aidan hesitated and Harry knew that he was a good man, that he didn't want to evict even a person like Jason Taylor, and then he told himself that Aidan had not known what Jason Taylor had been and in a way Harry was glad of it even though Aidan could not disguise that he thought little of a man who would do such a thing for another businessman and for apparently no reason but Aidan said nothing because he did not know and Harry admired that in him. What you did not know was very often the most important thing of all. And they both knew that.

Nineteen

'You didn't tell me Jason Taylor was going to be here,' Harry said to Ned as Ned took him into the drawing room some weeks later.

'Do you expect a list of my guests before you decide to attend my dinner?' Ned shot back at him.

'You know what I mean.'

'Your quarrels are not my problem. He is failing and you are watching him go down. It's not a pretty sight and not something a real gentleman would do.'

Harry was unused to Ned serious and offensive.

'I'm not a gentleman so it doesn't apply to me.'

He walked out of the room and down the hall towards the front door, unprepared for the way that Ned ran after him. Harry only hoped the other guests, grouped around the fire at the far end of the drawing room, did not notice.

'I didn't mean to say that.' Ned caught him by the arm as Harry reached the far end of the hall. Luckily it was deserted. He had been the last person to arrive. 'Annabel is worried about you, that's all, it isn't like you to behave like this and nobody understands why you're doing it.'

'There's no need to worry about me.'

'That's what I said to her, that you could take care of yourself, but she wouldn't have it and my father and Jason's father were friends. Don't walk out, you'll upset Annabel's very careful seating arrangements and she will kill me.'

Harry managed a smile at that.

'You can endure him for a couple of hours, surely, if he can endure you. You're not sitting next to him.' When Harry didn't move Ned said, 'Shona Rainbow is here. I know you've been friends for years and Annabel has seated you next to one another so she will have a spare seat next to her and that's rude, you know.'

Harry went back inside, followed by Ned who gave him a

generous glass of malt whisky and they went over to the fire
and Harry could see Shona so he went to her. He couldn't
think of anything to say. Luckily she didn't seem to notice as
there were other people nearby and she was talking to one
woman about the shop's progress. He thought she could probably talk about that all night.

Soon afterwards they went into dinner and the soup arrived.
Ned was right, Jason Taylor was not sitting next to him but
he was sitting across the table from Shona and he asked as they
began to eat how her shop was doing and when she answered
politely that she was hoping it would be a success he said that
he wished her well but was she sure that she shouldn't call it
something else.

'What do you mean?'

All of Harry's instincts yelled at him to get up, take Shona
by the hand and run out of there as fast as they could, like
some old Hansel and Gretel, he was made so unhappy by the
expression on Jason Taylor's face and the puzzled look on
Shona's.

'Shouldn't you call it Hardy's Emporium?'

'I did think about it because it was my father's idea first of
all and I wish he could have seen it now but Rainbow has
such a lovely sound to it.'

'Indeed, when one has the right to it.'

Shona gazed across the table. The soup was finished and
everybody was talking but there was a sudden silence.

'The right to what?' Shona said.

'To the name, such as you have not, have you?'

'Jason,' Ned broke in, 'please remember where you are.
Rivalry in business has no place here.'

'It's nothing to do with that, I'm just pointing out that Mrs
Rainbow is not Mrs Rainbow—'

'She was Mrs Rainbow for fifteen years,' Ned said.

'She was never Mrs Rainbow. She was nothing but James
Rainbow's whore.'

Harry didn't know how long it was before he took in this
information, he only knew that the silence which followed
was broken when he leaned over the table and did something
he had really wanted to do for years.

He hit Jason Taylor so hard in the face that the blood spurted all over Jason Taylor's evening shirt which of course was white so it made quite an impression, some woman shrieked and the crockery went everywhere and bounced or smashed when it hit the floor and best of all Jason Taylor went backwards and in Harry's mind it played slowly several times and he enjoyed each image.

So many people were instantly on their feet, Mrs Taylor's face was startled and full of horror. Harry could not believe what Jason Taylor had said but as he went over and over that in his head he knew that Taylor had deliberately set out to blacken Shona's reputation, had found information on her and Harry did not doubt that it was true and he could hardly think beyond it.

'For Christ's sake.' Ned tried to pull him away but somehow Harry had got across the table and had followed the assaulted man, pulled him up and knocked him on to the table, got him down there on the floor and did not intend to stop hitting him until he felt better. Ned and Aidan were there and they pulled him away. 'Will you leave it?' Ned banged him back against the wall and they held him until Harry stopped fighting to get back at the man.

'You get that bastard out of here,' was all Harry could manage, being short of breath by that time.

'This is all your fault,' Ned accused him. 'If you weren't so keen on bettering him things would never have come to this. He can't pay his damned bills, he can't keep his staff. Good people have lost their jobs and all because you are determined to make sure he fails spectacularly and in public.'

Ned moved back. The dining room was now empty. Annabel had escorted Shona out of the door. Other people were leaving, the hall was filled with quiet whispers and people finding their coats.

'I won't ever have him here again but he knows that Shona is your weakness,' Ned said when there was just the three of them.

'Oh, go and bugger yourself,' Harry said, launching himself away from the wall.

Aidan said nothing. He went after Lorna, who was waiting for him beyond the door.

Ned searched Harry's face for clues.

'Didn't you see what would happen, or didn't you care?'

'Stay out of this, Ned, it's none of your goddamned business,' Harry said and he went in search of Shona.

Annabel had taken her off to a little sitting room along the hall and Annabel was the one who looked up when Harry opened the door.

'I don't think—' she began.

Harry didn't look at her.

'Just leave us,' he said.

'But—'

He looked appealingly at her. Annabel went out, shutting the door quietly behind her. Shona hadn't looked up. She was white-faced and half turned away and the fire made her hair look even redder than it was.

'You didn't marry him?'

'No, I didn't.'

'Why not?' He kept the questions soft so that she would answer.

'I had no choice in that, he wouldn't marry me.'

'Because?'

She turned away altogether, in a hopeless gesture.

'Because he was supposed to marry some other girl, somebody he'd been betrothed to since he was a small child. After he took me to the village and told them he wouldn't have her his family never spoke to him again or me either.'

'Then why didn't he marry you?'

'I don't know. I think he thought that in time they would come round, that everything would be all right, but it never was. And there was no child, I think if there had been then – it hurt him so very much, he denied it but it did. I think he thought he could go back there and everything would be all right.

'It didn't really matter, she married another lad in the end – she had no choice, she had to marry somebody, but she always wanted James – and he had gone too far, broken the rules. We couldn't set foot in the church because his mother and the rest of the family went there, I think that had a lot to do with the reason why we weren't married.'

'You couldn't move away—'

'He wouldn't go, he was like somebody haunted, part of him wanted to leave, to break free, but he couldn't, he wanted to be forgiven, he wanted us to be part of his family. The only time I set foot inside their church was for his funeral and even then I was scorned. Women didn't go to funerals there, they weren't supposed to, they were supposed to stay at home and brew tea and make sandwiches. In some places women never get beyond the – the tea and the – the sandwiches.'

The way that she faltered made Harry aware of how upset she was. Her hands shook on her lap. He sighed.

'Why didn't you come home?'

'After going away like that?'

'Your father always thought you would come back.'

'I didn't even know he was dead.' She turned and looked at Harry for the first time. 'You could have found me, made a real attempt, I mean.'

'I thought you were happy.'

'We were very happy. I should have cared that we weren't married and I did but it didn't matter. Nothing on earth could have prevented me from staying with him, being with him day by day. It was wonderful. I didn't know you could love someone as much as that. I wanted him more than I had wanted anything in my whole life. I wouldn't give up a second of it for society's so-called respectability.'

Nobody spoke for a short while and then she smiled at him and she said, 'Thank you for looking after my father, I feel like I bought my freedom with yours, and thank you for what you did to Jason Taylor.'

'I brought him down on you,' Harry admitted.

'I don't care, and if people judge me and stay away I don't care about that either. Marriage is a stupid idea anyway.'

Harry smiled at that.

'Would you like to get out of here?'

'I would love it,' she said.

'Let's go back to my hotel and have dinner.'

'So very publicly.'

'Why yes, why not?'

★   ★   ★

Shona regretted her decision immediately but it was somehow
the only way she could think of to get out of there. She wanted
to run away and hide, she could not believe that she had
deceived these people who had tried to be her friends but
then what else could she do? How could she have hidden what
she had felt for James all those years? How could she have
made something up which was nothing to do with her as an
explanation as to why she had come back to Durham? What
could she have said, that she had been away and not been
married and not been with him? What else could she have
done? She could not think.

It was Harry's calm manner which she dared say he used
very often on his customers when they were nearing hysteria
or whatever it was she was nearing that got her out of there.
He was in professional mode, it would have made her smile
had she not wanted to disappear and cry so badly.

The stupid thing about it was that she had forgotten she
was not married. After a while, after she had threatened to
leave him and been unable to, it did not seem to matter.
Nobody spoke to them anyhow and if she went into Alnwick
where she was not known she was Mrs Rainbow to the shopkeepers and anybody she dealt with, she had to be. She wished
she could have said to Harry that she had tried to leave James,
God knew she had tried to leave him a dozen times but she
was physically incapable of such a thing and he was aware of
it.

He loved her, he told her so often, but he would not marry
her, because of his family. She could not change his mind and
that was that. She could make no better of it while she stayed
with him, her choices were to stay or to go as she chose. The
simplicity of it was that there was nowhere in the world she
wanted to be without him.

As they reached Harry's car outside she stopped and said, 'I
think I would just like to go home. Would you mind?'

'Not at all.'

The journey in the silence seemed endless and she was only
glad when they reached the shop but even now the name in the
darkness seemed to jump out at her and accuse her of lies and
stupidity and she thanked him very quickly and got down

and would not let him help her and ran away into the shop and up the stairs and into her own room without seeing anybody and there she began to cry and could not stop for a very long time.

She did not sleep. She tried to decide what to do next. She was caught in her own deception. She began to wish now that she had taken Jason Taylor's offer and the money and left and gone somewhere new and that would have been better though when she thought about it very hard she could not envisage where she might go and everywhere she went people would find out and she would be no better off. How far would she have had to go to get away from it all? Would she ever have been happy? She doubted it.

She tried to work out whether to tell Mrs Robson and Mr Simpson and Gino but every time she went over it in her mind it sounded so bad that she thought they would leave straight away if they could and if they could not they would stay where they were and despise her. She did not want to see anybody but she could not stay in her room later than usual or they would think she was ill so she pretended that everything was all right.

Annabel came to see her that morning, Shona was horrified. She said she was too busy. Annabel said, 'I think we should talk about this,' as they hurried through the new part of the building, on the first floor. Nobody else was there and Shona was not only glad of that because she didn't want anybody to overhear anything but also wished things the other way round because she didn't even want to look at Annabel.

'I'm sorry I spoiled your party,' she said and hurried away but Annabel ran after her.

'You have to try and sort this out,' she said.

Shona ignored her.

'I'm thinking of putting linen, curtains and furniture up here, though the furniture would be better downstairs, because of all the lifting, especially when people buy it.'

'Shona, please.'

'I said I don't have time.'

Annabel held her arm as Shona tried to get away so she stopped and turned, remembering how kind this woman had been to her.

'What on earth is it you think I can do?' she said finally.

'I don't know but you must do something because once word gets around in such a small city no one will come to the shop any more and there will be a huge scandal and only disreputable people will come any more and you will end up—' Annabel stopped there.

'Like my father? Failing?'

'Something like that, yes.'

'Do you have a suggestion?'

'That you let Jason Taylor have the shop—'

'At a reduced price? After the way that he treated me? Because that's what he will do.'

'I don't think you have any choice, I don't think you can stay here.'

'In that case I don't think I want to stay here. Why don't you go back to your beautiful house and your elegant husband and your gorgeous children and leave me alone?'

'I'm not judging you, Shona, I wouldn't do that, but other people will and they care about such things. It may seem very stupid—'

'But it's the way that society is put together, I know,' Shona said bitterly, 'and people who flout its rules are put out into the cold. I would have married him if I had had the choice but he made it impossible for us to be married and I couldn't leave him and to be frank, Annabel, I fail to see why society revolves around such a ridiculous set of rules.'

Annabel was right. Very soon people stopped coming to the shop. Within a week Shona was losing money. None of the staff left but they all knew and by the end of the week when they sat down to have a meal in the early evening Mr Simpson got up from the table, coughed and said, 'I have something to say on behalf of us all.' Everybody had stopped talking. Nobody was looking at her. Shona wanted to run out of the room. 'We don't understand what is going on but we know that you must have had a very good reason for what you did. You have been kind to us when nobody else would and we are not going anywhere without you.'

Gino was nodding. Mrs Robson and the girls looked hopefully at her.

'I wanted to tell you,' Shona said, 'but there were no words to suit it somehow. I'm afraid that the shop will not make any money and you will be on the streets.'

'People will forget,' Mrs Robson said, 'and others won't care.'

It was comforting but Shona could not eat and she knew when she went to bed that this was not true and she lay there and wondered what it would be like when she had to sell the shop to Jason Taylor – if he would take it now. Perhaps he would not. She decided that she must make an appointment to see Aidan Hedley as soon as she could and no matter what Mr Taylor offered her for the shop she must take it and see that everybody was all right.

The following morning when she was keeping busy upstairs making plans which she thought would never come to fruition and feeling so bad that she could hardly stand up she heard a slight noise behind her and when she turned Harry was standing there.

'I've made an appointment to see Aidan Hedley,' she said, 'I have no choice. I hate to let Mr Taylor win but there's nothing else I can do.'

'There's always an alternative,' he said.

She looked at him and she thought that his face was inscrutable. He hadn't been like that before, as though he was withdrawing more and more into himself, and becoming less and less readable even for somebody like her who thought she knew him so well.

'You don't want him to have it?'

'Less now than ever.'

'I don't think that's true. I don't think you ever meant him to have my shop. You could have bought it yourself but of course you had no use for it until he wanted it. What is it about him that you dislike so much? I feel like a pawn.'

'We could get married.'

Shona didn't think she could be surprised any more. As it was she almost fell over. She stared at him, gained nothing from it and said bluntly, 'Are you mad?'

'You could keep the shop.'

'And rename it Mrs Darling's Emporium? Don't be silly.'

She walked away, down the stairs and through the almost

empty shop and into her office. That little room always comforted her but now the sparrows and dunnocks were startled at her quick movement and flew away as one. Harry had followed her.

'Please go away. I have things to do.'

'You have nothing to do, at least you'll soon have nothing to do,' he said smoothly.

Shona tried to think. She sat down behind her desk, that always made her feel in charge.

'You couldn't marry me. What about your own reputation?'

'Everybody owes me money,' he said.

That made her laugh. Then she became grave.

'It's an absolutely stupid idea and you know it is and I don't think even you would do that because you want Jason Taylor to fail and if you are doing it because of what I did for you then that's an even worse reason and worst of all is the fact that I don't care for you in that way. I never did.'

There was a very awkward pause from her suitor and Shona stole a glance at him only to find that he was not looking at her.

'I don't care about all that,' he said, 'I'm not going to ask you to sleep with me.'

For some reason, at that point, all Shona could remember was the one night they had gone dancing. When they had been close he had not tried to hold her any nearer. She hadn't thought about it then, hadn't known that men did so, that James would never have let her go, would never have gone calmly back and slept in the same room in a separate bed and somehow things were worse than that.

She was not sure whether she had made them so by going off, by leaving Harry, by adding what could have been bitterness and resentment and even perhaps hate. He was right, he was not offering her passion or even love, he was offering her the shop and she was offering him – was she offering him Jason Taylor, was she giving over to him some kind of power over another man? She had the awful feeling that it was not a thing you should ever do.

He was dangerous, she thought, she had never thought so

before but her instincts told her so. There was something about Harry which would lead her into deep water. Then she wanted to laugh. When had any man offered her anything regular or ordinary? Why should she hesitate now? She had a great deal to lose by the shop and if she sold it to Jason Taylor – and she was not sure she could let herself do that and leave – she felt as though her life would be so compromised by men that she would never want anything to do with any of them again.

'Could we have a house?'

'Yes.'

'And could I have my own rooms?'

'Anything you want.'

'And you wouldn't try to take the shop from me?'

'Why would I do that?' He looked at her, possibly for the first time since he had suggested they should marry.

'I don't see the advantage in it for you.'

'I don't want Taylor to have the shop and I don't want you to leave. I never wanted you to leave.'

This was true.

'We were always good friends,' he said, 'when you left I lost the best part of my day, the coming home in the evening and sitting around the fire, talking.'

She had not lost that, she thought, James had been like Harry that way, his favourite time of day was when the world was shut out, the door was locked, the sweet-smelling wood from the beach was alight with flame and there was just the two of them but she thought with some bitterness now that it was too exclusive a world to hold together when something went wrong and it had crashed and died with James. Harry was more like James than she had thought, he did not care much for other people, he did not encourage their company.

'All right then,' she said, 'I'll do it.' There was no alternative that she could bear. She was not sure she could bear this.

Twenty

Harry procured a special licence and they were married a few days later in St Nicholas's Church in the Market Place. Annabel and Ned, Gina, Mr Simpson and Mrs Robson and the two girls attended. The two girls were excited about the idea of somebody getting married and that they would be there so Shona tried to enter into their enthusiasm and backed by the idea of all Harry's money she went out and bought new clothes for the girls and Mrs Robson and herself from the expensive dress shop near Elvet Bridge. Harry bought new suits for Gino and Mr Simpson, hastily made at the tailoring department in Shona's shop.

Harry ordered a private room at the County Hotel and they had lunch there after the ceremony and champagne and cake.

'That,' said Annabel Fleming to her husband as they made their way home, 'was the strangest wedding I ever attended. The bride looked like she wanted to run away and the groom didn't speak except when he had to.'

They had not talked about what would happen after the wedding. If Harry had owned a house she could have gone there with him though she would much rather have stayed on at the shop. She had grown used to the people who worked for her and there the talk was always of new ideas and she liked how they sat around in the evenings and she knew that she would miss it.

As it was she must go and stay at the hotel with Harry. She was most reluctant to go anywhere with him, it felt so wrong, so strange, she was already regretting what she thought of as the most stupidly impulsive thing she had ever done. There must be no more talk however so they stayed at the hotel.

Her newly purchased suitcase contained clothes hastily bought from the shop within her own store and the little shop on Elvet Bridge and were more suited to the bank owner's wife. These were carried upstairs and she saw her new quarters and was astonished at the luxury.

It was three rooms – four if you counted the bathroom. A bathroom. She gazed at it and at the spacious living room with its French windows which overlooked the river and the bedrooms, one at either side of the sitting room, and she thought of the last house where she and Harry had lived together, in Paradise Lane, and she longed for the little cottage where she had lived with James.

The bedrooms each had a big double bed, wardrobes, dressing table, even easy chairs, and the sitting room had big sofas, bookcases full of what she presumed were Harry's books, and little tables and large reading lamps and all three rooms had fires so that they would be cosy enough when the weather was bad.

Harry was obviously using the sitting room partly as an office but said he would move papers and desk into his bedroom if she preferred and she said she didn't mind since she would be at the shop most of the time and he said he stayed at the bank, coming back at eight, and did she think that she might come back and eat dinner with him sometimes and Shona said that yes, of course she would and she wondered at how she and Harry who had once been so close were now so awkward in one another's presence.

They sat down and he asked if she would like more champagne and she said she was dying for some tea so he rang down for this and they watched the sun go down and she tried and failed to think of anything reasonably sensible to say and when the tea was drunk her mouth took on a life of its own and she said, 'I'm still not sure this was a good idea,' and he said: 'Neither am I,' and then she smiled at him in relief somehow that they thought alike on the matter and he was not afraid to admit it.

'You could have said before now,' she said.

'I didn't like to. I couldn't come up with a reasonable alternative. I didn't want you to leave Durham again.'

'What about Jason Taylor?' She thought of how kind Mrs Taylor had been to her when she went to the house and how awful she had felt when she went in and she wondered whether the atmosphere of the place would change when they left it.

'You don't need to worry about him any more. He'll be leaving his house over the next few days and his store will be closing down so yours is almost certain to be successful, there being no other competition.'

Shona wasn't sure she liked the implied idea, that she might only be successful without anyone else there, she wasn't afraid of competition but it didn't help to say so.

'Somebody else might buy it.'

Harry said nothing and then she understood.

'You've taken that too, haven't you? What will you do with it?'

'I don't know yet but a place this size doesn't need two department stores and it has been losing money for a very long time.'

'And the house?' A horrible thought occurred to her. 'You don't want us to live there, do you?'

Harry looked curiously at her.

'Do you know the place?'

'I went to look at it, to see what all the fuss was about, and Mrs Taylor came past and asked me inside for tea. She was very kind but – I didn't like the atmosphere. I suppose if they have left the atmosphere might change but it was more than the people in it somehow and there was nothing wrong with her, I thought she was a very nice woman, and the place was furnished with taste and simplicity and his personality alone could not have caused it to feel so – so dark. I don't know what it was but I didn't care for it.'

Harry said nothing but that he had no desire to live there and Shona was amazed at herself that she had thought there was anything left of the boy she had known, her slight acquaintance with Harry since she had come back had not prepared her for the long silences which followed. She began to wish she had not eaten so much earlier and said, 'Do you think we could go down to dinner?'

'Yes, of course, if you wish.'

'It isn't that I'm hungry but I have so many new frocks to air,' she said lightly and each of them went off into the bedroom to change and she was so glad to be by herself that she stood against the door for a few seconds, unhappy with what she had done.

They duly went into the dining room and everybody who was there turned to see. She took her lead from Harry and ignored them and went to sit down and felt much better when she had drunk a very large Martini. She had never had a Martini before and was quite surprised at how it altered her mood. She had to remind herself that her father had been a drunk when Harry offered to order her another and shook her head.

'I'd have to go to bed if I had another,' she said but she did not stop him from ordering wine with the meal.

They ate lightly and she was glad of the full dining room, the hum of other people's conversation somehow covered the lack of talk between them and it did not pass her by that they had the best table in the dining room beside the window and well away from other people's ears had they had anything intimate they wished to discuss.

All through the meal she thought back to the way that she had gone off to Northumberland with James and what the first night had been like, how she had not been able to stop herself from wanting him more than she had wanted anything or anyone in the whole of her young life. She did not want Harry at all and by the look of him he did not want her either.

After a large glass of something white which had seemed so innocuous when she began it she asked him a question she could not help.

'Did you ever fall in love?'

He didn't seem very surprised but then he had cultivated a perfect banker's expression which stopped everything in front of it with a general bland look.

'No, I didn't.'

'And you aren't in love with me now?'

'Did you want dessert?'

'So you weren't in love with me when I left Paradise Lane?'

'I missed you very much, I missed your conversation, and the day-to-day stuff which I dare say most people are satisfied with—'

'But it wasn't love?'

'I am and always was very fond of you.'

'Heavens, what a conversation, I don't think I ought to have any more wine.'

'It doesn't matter. Nobody can hear.'

'And you don't mind?'

'Of course not.'

There was something so bloodless about it all that Shona became very tired and was grateful when it was late enough to leave the dining room and she was even more grateful that Harry had had the foresight to realize that she would need her own room but when she was safely in bed she could not help let fall a good many tears for the young man who would never come back to her.

She felt so wrong in every way, the only thing she was glad about was that she would not have to go through this farce of a wedding again the next day but it seemed so awful that she could not marry the man she had wanted to marry and instead had married a man she did not wish to be married to.

Shona had the sign changed on the shop so that it read The Rainbow Emporium and was half satisfied with that and from the very beginning she spent as much time as she could at work. She was able to get rid of the cheap ring she had bought for herself half in shame in a tiny second-hand goods shop in a back street in Alnwick but she wasn't sure she preferred it to the platinum band which Harry had fitted on to her finger. He had also offered to buy her a diamond for her finger but she had had enough sense to turn that down. What was the point in pretending?

She thought a good deal about James during the days which followed and missed him more and more but Harry had been right about the business, as soon as she married him people began to come back into the shop. She hated them for having judged her in that way and herself for caring but the shop had become the most important thing in her life.

There were some good things attached to the marriage. Unlike James, Harry never ever told her what to do or questioned how she spent money and she hadn't known until then that James did. She had loved him so much that she hadn't minded either that their tastes were different and their ideas.

She hadn't cared at the time but she did like the look of expensive clothes on her by now slender figure, she liked the feel of good cloth and also the idea that Harry didn't care what she bought. She didn't consult him about her ideas for the shop, he provided money for that when she needed it.

If she asked him for his opinion he would put the question back to her, she began to think that Harry would have made a very good teacher, he enabled her to do the things she wanted and with confidence and very soon she found that she would go over to the bank where he was working at around seven and they would walk back to the hotel together and spend the meal talking about work just as they always had.

Sometimes he went away for a night to see other banks in various parts of the county and she missed him and she learned to like Sundays. She was aware that he had always worked on Sundays but she didn't and when it was fine they went walking by the river and they even talked about the old days, about Julius and the market and about her father and the house in Paradise Lane.

Sometimes they drove up to Newcastle and stayed overnight in a hotel and went to the theatre there and other times they motored into Weardale and spent the fine days by the river, stopping off at a tea shop for afternoon tea.

They ventured further, he took her to London on the train and then to Paris. It wasn't ever for long, he didn't like to leave the banks and she didn't like to leave the shop. It was only some months later, when they were having dinner with Annabel and Ned and several friends, and Shona saw herself in a huge Venetian mirror which was one of two in Annabel's drawing room that she stopped and stared.

She was wearing pearls around her neck and in her ears, her black dress had cost a fortune, there was a diamond ring on her finger – she had long since given in to such things. Her hair was swept up and held with a pearl clip and her shoes had been made for her.

She was a rich man's wife and not just that, the shop was doing well, she was opening up different departments, and better than that she and Harry had plans for the other store and she was excited and they would sit and talk for hours, in the same way, stupidly, as they had in the evenings at Paradise

Lane and when she turned and looked at her husband now it was as though she was seeing him so differently.

He was the most attractive man in the room. How odd. She had never thought so before, it had not occurred to her. They all looked good, they were rich young men, they were wearing evening dress and she liked Ned because he made Harry laugh and the meal was over.

Annabel had stopped taking her women friends off to drink tea, she hated it, she said, so the men had their port and their cigars and the women sat there too and smoked and drank coffee – and brandy or port if they wished – and did whatever they wanted.

Harry was relaxed. He wasn't often like that but she knew he felt safe here with Ned and Aidan, who were his real friends. She couldn't hear what they were saying, it was obviously a discussion of something light, not business, something silly as men did about sport, and she saw Ned look across the table at his wife and he winked at her. It wasn't something anybody else was meant to see but she felt a pang of jealousy that they had such a wonderful relationship.

Aidan was married now. His wife wore a lovely silver grey dress and she looked very happy but Harry didn't notice Shona, she could tell, he was completely absorbed in the conversation and she wished that he would just look up, sense her, but although she watched him he didn't and she couldn't help admiring how he looked, the slender hands which held the cigar and how his expensive clothes made his body look so desirable. She thought she had definitely had too much to drink.

Annabel was talking about one of her friends who had married a little while back for the second time.

'She had given up on the idea of a child and you know how difficult that is but you know what. She's pregnant.'

Shona stared at her friend.

'But she was married previously for years.'

'She's almost forty. She was married to Bill for twelve years and nothing happened. He was a very nice man but they were so upset when they couldn't have a child. Now she's been married to Philip for just a year. Isn't that wonderful?'

Shona had to agree that it was and it was not for some moments that she thought Annabel was trying to tell her something and she wasn't sure whether to laugh or cry. She could not tell her friend that hers was not that kind of marriage, it wasn't really any kind of a marriage at all but it had been successful so far because they both knew what they wanted and what they wanted had worked out.

Shona had not considered the idea of having a child with Harry but when they went back to the County, she couldn't help thinking about what Annabel had said. Exactly what her friend had no doubt intended, Shona thought, mentally cursing her.

She had wanted her child to be James's because they had loved one another. Harry did love her but it was not that kind of thing at all, it was friendly and generous but there was something about him which held everybody, even herself, at a distance and she did not know how to cover that distance between them, she had not wanted to, she wasn't sure whether she ever would want it but the question remained.

She lay awake for most of the night and the following day the more she tried to put from her mind the idea of a child the less successful she was and she cursed the instinct that led her there. She worked very hard so that she would have no time to think. Harry however was too shrewd a man not to realize that there was something wrong.

'What's on your mind?' he asked, when they went down to drink Martini before dinner. She had by now grown used to this and looked forward to that time and she liked living in the hotel because she could wear lovely dresses but that night she didn't care about any of it, it seemed so unimportant, so shallow, as though her whole life was on show for other people, as though it was a sham.

She denied there was anything the matter and thought then how respectful he was of what she said. He would not pursue it unless she allowed him to. His great talent was to give people room to be who they were or who they wanted to be.

They got halfway through the dessert when she put down her spoon and fork and said, 'Have you ever wanted to have children?'

Harry stopped too but he took in the question, said, 'No,' and went on to finish the caramel custard.

'Is it because you don't like children?'

He didn't answer that.

'I don't think I ever met anybody who didn't like children.'

'Oh, I don't think that's the worry, the real worry is people who do. Who in their right minds could care for the little beggars?'

Shona was rather taken aback at the vehemence with which he said this and didn't understand.

'You like Ned and Annabel's children.'

'That's because they're theirs and I don't have to put up with them except when they're on their best behaviour.'

'I would have liked to have a child to James.'

'I'm sure you would but in the circumstances it's perhaps just as well that you didn't.'

'That's a horrible thing to say to me.'

'Is it?' He looked quickly at her. 'I'm sorry, I didn't think.'

The coffee arrived. Shona had a terrible desire to cry and sat there, as she must, hurt and feeling rejected. She knew how silly it was but she couldn't help it.

'People would have found out that you weren't married and your child was illegitimate. Then what would you have done and how awful would it have been for that child? You must know,' Harry persisted.

'I have no idea,' she shot back at him and she glared across the table at him. 'I would have lied for my child, nobody would have known, I would have done everything in my power to protect him. I wouldn't have let anybody hurt him.'

Harry looked at her and she thought it was possibly the warmest look he had given her since they had met again.

'I know you would,' he said. 'I didn't mean to upset you, Shona. Forgive me?'

'I would like some brandy,' she said.

'So would I. Why don't we ask them to bring the coffee and brandy upstairs?'

She was thankful to leave the dining room and that the fire in their sitting room had been built up, all three fires had been, and she had never grown used to the idea that things would be done for her comfort that she did not have to do for herself. The brandy and the coffee soothed her. It was a cold dark night, the wind whistled around the town and down the chimney but she was safely inside. The brandy was poured into great big balloon glasses. She liked these, she liked the way that the brandy warmed under her hand.

'Are you sorry we got married?' he said, at length.

'No, I got what I wanted, more than I wanted really, and I don't want your child, I just feel the lack because of James and I just wanted to say it. I understand the agreement and I'm sure you have good reasons for how you go on. I think I shall go to bed now.'

He wished her goodnight and she went, stumbling because she couldn't see for tears. She thought he didn't notice.

The Monday of that week was very busy. Shona loved her shop and she loved the idea that everybody, no matter what their income or circumstances, could find something to buy and they could sit in the cafe and have nothing more than a cheap cup of coffee. Lots of women came in from the cold and the dreariness of the back streets and sat there for hours and her staff had instructions to turn away no one but those who were troublemakers. She had hired a young Scotsman, not particularly tall or menacing but he was what Ned and Harry called 'a hard man' and if there was any trouble he took care of it without fuss.

In the cafe she had provided toys for the children and if the odd little girl went off with a doll or a train disappeared nobody said anything. Those who stole for anything more than themselves were well known and watched so she was happy with the shop's progress.

She felt strange on the day that she was given the keys to the other shop, she and Harry having decided she would run it, after weeks of discussion about what they might do with it.

To have won so sweepingly was not a comfortable feeling and it was worse when later, the ideas tumbling one on top of another in her mind, she wandered back to her office through the front door just to make sure everybody was busy, she saw a slight figure off to the side and looked twice.

It was Mrs Taylor. She barely recognized her. The woman had lost so much weight, her clothes were worn and her whole figure was weary. She didn't look in Shona's direction, Shona was convinced that Mrs Taylor just happened to be going by. The day was cold but her coat was thin and Shona wanted to duck inside, to ignore her, to pretend that she hadn't seen the consequences of what she and Harry had done and it wouldn't matter, her worse self told her, Mrs Taylor hadn't seen her, she wasn't looking up. She hadn't looked up in a long time, Shona thought.

She went over.

'Mrs Taylor?'

It was several seconds before the woman even lifted her head and during the months since they had last met at the dinner party where Harry hit her husband she had aged so much that she was quite different. There were huge lines which divided her cheeks. Her eyes were dull, her hair was lifeless and devoid of colour and sprouting from her hat and there was no anger, no resentment, only recognition.

'Why, Mrs Darling, how are you?' Her voice was croaky as though she didn't need to use it often but her tone was just the same, friendly and refined and sounded so wrong against the way that she looked.

'Will you come in and have coffee?'

'I had better not.'

'Oh, do, please.'

Mrs Taylor hesitated and then looked at the doors of the shop and longing came into her eyes at the idea of warmth and comfort, Shona could see. Shona guided her inside, took her into the office, sat her down by the warm fire and gave a cup of strong coffee into her hands as soon as it arrived and she had asked for a plate of warm pastries and after hesitating as Shona offered the plate to her Mrs Taylor accepted one, white with fondant icing, and ate it daintily as though she wasn't really hungry and after that she ate another. After sipping her own coffee Shona said, 'I meant to tell you that I was so sorry for what happened.'

Shona felt awful.

'It wasn't your fault,' Mrs Taylor said. She sighed and sat back in her chair and began to look more like herself. 'We are not to blame for what men do or for the way that society is so organized that we have no place in it other than as wives. I shouldn't have married him though I had very little choice in the matter, I needed to marry for all kinds of reasons. I have regretted it ever since.'

Shona thought it was something a great many women could have said.

'We were never happy. He always—' She faltered. 'He always had other women, he was so difficult to live with and now he's gone off and left me.'

'Left you?'

'I have no idea where he went. I did go and stay with Elspeth and her husband and they were very kind but they've just got married. You cannot imagine how difficult it is to watch other people happy. How awful that sounds. The thing is that I know how fleeting happiness can be, I wouldn't spoil it for them while it lasts.' She finished the coffee, Shona poured more.

'I never liked that house,' Mrs Taylor said. 'It was Jason who wanted to be there. It was far too big and sometimes had an atmosphere I couldn't stand. I had to pretend for so many years. At least I don't have to do that any more.'

'Do you have somewhere to stay?'

'Oh yes, I – I have a room.'

The room was in a downtrodden hotel in a back street, Shona recognized the place which her guest described.

'Would you stay here with us?' Shona offered.

'My dear, you can't take in everybody.'

'You aren't everybody. Let's go and get your things.'

After that Mrs Taylor talked openly.

'He only married me because I came from a good family, what a stupid idea that is, "good", they were fools, they lost all their money because they were stupid and then he went and did the same. I wished I could have helped but he didn't think it seemly. I was quite good at needlework when I was a young girl. I longed to do embroidery, just some peace and a few books.' She laughed and suddenly looked much younger. 'I wasn't allowed to do things like that, books and things like needlework were for lesser people, I had to ride to hounds and listen all evening to people bleating on about the chase. Oh, it was tedious, you cannot imagine.'

Shona laughed. She had not thought Mrs Taylor had a sense of humour or exercised it even when times were this bad.

'Do you do embroidery now?'

'It's the only thing that brings me comfort.'

'Why don't we go upstairs and have a look at the haberdashery department? I could do with someone who has some knowledge of such things, I have no idea about them and neither has anybody else. I have a young girl on there at the moment and she's very willing but she isn't very deft.'

Mrs Taylor let herself be guided and Shona watched her once she got there, her eyes lit over the different coloured silks, the needles, the patterns on the material which were guides for the embroiderer and she said, and it was heaven to Shona's ears, 'I always wanted to design my own patterns, to weave in my own ideas and see them on people's chairs.' She laughed. 'Fancy wanting to have patterns for something on which people sit. How ridiculous.'

That evening Shona was so busy that she didn't get over the road to the bank before she saw Harry making his way out of the door and she thought again how pleasant it would be for them to go back to somewhere which was theirs, with their own furniture, something where food didn't automatically happen – she was ashamed to think it but she was tired of the menu at the County Hotel. Sometimes they went to other places but she wanted to be in charge of her own kitchen, the food and the crockery.

Harry wanted to hear her ideas for the new shop but she was a little afraid, she didn't know why, to tell him that she had taken on Mrs Taylor.

'And she's staying there too,' she said, a trifle defiantly.

Harry looked uncomfortable. He was looking back at her through the mirror in his bedroom, trying to tie his evening tie.

'Let me do that,' she said and she realized then that she

always had to, he could never do it and she had become expert in such a short time. 'Did you know that Jason Taylor had left?'

The tie successfully tied Harry moved away. He didn't say anything and that was unusual. He was good at answering questions and for all he had been brought up in the back streets, she thought, he was too polite not to do so if he had any answer to give that was reasonable. Shona tried again.

'Harry, she's all alone.'

'Not now, I take it. You've ensconced her in your hotel for strays and she has a married daughter she could go to.'

'You think I shouldn't have taken her in?'

'No, I think you were right and in any case it doesn't matter what I think, what you do at the shop is your business.'

'It matters to me what you think,' she said. 'There are so many things that you don't say and—' Shona couldn't imagine what came after that.

'How could I say that you shouldn't take in anybody? If it hadn't been for you I would have been dead at thirteen. It's the most wonderful thing of all about you,' he said.

'Wonderful?'

'Very wonderful,' he said.

Shona felt quite shaky.

'Apart from "I love you" I think that's the nicest thing anybody ever said to me.'

She heard him hesitate and then more than that, pause and stand back just a little and then he said softly, 'Jason Taylor is dead.'

Harry spent quite a lot of time with Ned and Aidan. None of them had taken off much time before now but suddenly he thought they wearied of work and over the past few weeks had taken to meeting in a pub in Saddler Street, the winding road which went up to the cathedral. It was called the Shakespeare and inside it was a number of tiny rooms running into one another so that you could be quite private there, nobody would know you were sitting at the back of the place and it was gloomy and quiet and Harry had grown used to it. It was their escape.

And it was here that they had talked about Dragon's Field and what should be done with it. Ned, never one to dodge a difficult subject, had said, after his second pint of beer, 'So what are you going to do with the place, having gotten rid of the family?'

Harry was aware that Ned didn't agree with what he had done. Aidan had given no opinion and was silent now. They had another pint and at the end of it they decided because they had some time that afternoon to go across to Dragon's Field and look around. Why not?

Harry thought he would feel differently in that place with his two friends, they were enough to help anyone and with beer inside him he felt courageous enough to go there, to open it up, and it was a cold bright day and afternoon sun was doing its best before it set to turn the building to gold. He did not hesitate in opening the front door but once inside, almost empty of furniture, the noise of their footsteps echoed and it was worse than that, he wanted to run outside. There was a smell which was not unlike a butcher's somehow.

'What the hell is that?' Ned asked and unafraid of anything he plunged into the hall, opened various big doors and when he came to the dining room he went inside, the smell increasing and then he said, 'Oh, God,' and backed out of there.

Aidan was not so squeamish, it was part of his job to accept whatever he found, so he went forward as Ned retreated and Harry went with him.

Jason Taylor was hanging in the room.

'He'd been there for some time,' Harry said now, 'there were signs he'd been living there, he'd built a fire and there was food and wine and – blankets and such. We got the police of course and there will be an inquest—'

'And Mrs Taylor?'

'She will be told now that they know where she is,' Harry said.

'How she must hate us. She won't stay.'

'It has nothing to do with you. If you talk to her—'

'What on earth am I supposed to say?' She looked hard at him, Harry wasn't looking at her, or at anything else really.

'I'm terribly sorry my husband drove yours to suicide but if you really want we'll find you some embroidery to do? Very nice, I don't think.' She looked at him again but he was calm. 'Aren't you sorry at all?'

He didn't answer her. Shona was so angry and a lot of that anger was because she couldn't understand how he could be that vindictive, she didn't recognize it in him and was very disappointed. Suddenly it was as if all the sophistication fell away from him and he was just another grubby boy from the streets and she was sorry for the first time that she had taken somebody in. In the years that they had been apart he had changed.

'How can you do that?' she said. 'How could you do such a thing?'

Ned had said almost exactly the same thing only in less polite terms, had raged and shouted and told Harry he had thought he knew him and now it was obviously not true and how horrified Annabel would be and how on earth would he tell Shona and that Harry had driven a man to his death. All Harry could think was that it was so obvious Ned was a newspaper man, he spoke in headlines all the time.

When the police had been and the body taken away and all traces of Jason Taylor were gone he made himself go back once again. He went to the dark passage where the cupboard had existed during years he had lived there and he discovered that it was in fact a very small room, without any window.

He shone light in there but couldn't make himself go inside and he realized that this was why he was so afraid of small dark places, of the possibility of being closed inside with the door slammed and no way of getting out. He had conquered this feeling over the years without quite knowing why he avoided crowded meeting places such as theatres.

He was all right in a box, now that he was rich he could avoid other people, but he could remember being stuck in the middle of a row and the theatre dark and that strange awful feeling coming over him. It wasn't physical in a sense, that was the stupid part but it appeared so. A cough would rise in his throat until he could not stop and it would make an excuse for him to get out so that the production whatever it was would not be interrupted but he had known after a while that the moment he was outside it stopped.

Other places, art galleries, restaurants, were the same, strange really when it was the shut inside alone which had started this off and it meant that he had long since decided that people could not put up with him and why should they?

Only his long regard for Shona had got him this far to her. Further than that he could not go and now it seemed he needed to back off even further and never come out of the nightmare that was endless time in that tiny space where he was locked in. His breath came short and suddenly he couldn't breathe at all and the next thing he knew there was blackness even greater than the tiny room and when he came to he was lying on the floor in the hall. He had passed out.

The lamp thankfully was upright and still burning and so he got up and made himself go inside, fearing that he might get to the stage where he couldn't breathe again but he didn't. His breathing was just as it should be once it got back to being regular.

There wasn't much to explore but in the farthest corner he found a small wooden object and the light showed him that it was a train, a child's toy, the colour rubbed off it, the dirt showed its age. He felt sick. There was too a broken doll, how stupidly poignant that was, china, its arms and legs broken, its blue unseeing eyes staring out endlessly into the darkness.

Shona didn't come back to the hotel that evening and when he went to the shop he found lights blazing not just where the residents were living but in her office and as he reached it she heard him and when he saw her she avoided his eyes.

'I think I might stay here for a while.'

He understood. He said nothing but, 'All right,' and then he went back to the hotel.

He hired a gang of men to pull down the house at Dragon's Field and he went there every day at some time to watch until the whole thing was finished, until there was nothing but an enormous pile of bricks and stone, when you could see clearly to the horizon.

It made him feel so much better. He walked among the

ruins, watching the men digging up the gardens, breathing the clear air, glad to be outside, reluctant to go back to town where he knew people were judging him. The invitations had already dried up. Miss Piers need no longer come in during the day and ask him whether he wanted to go to this party or that gathering. She said nothing, she remained constant but she was the only one.

His staff were silent as they must be so he got on with his work and he went home in the evening and ate upstairs in his room and to his surprise he began to sleep better than he had ever done in his life and in his dreams the house at Dragon's Field had turned into something more, something positive, and all the bad things about it had gone and the feelings were almost gone, they were draining away like puddles in cornfields when the hot afternoon sun obliterated them.

Despite what Shona had said and thought Mrs Taylor stayed with her. She did not seem very affected by her husband's death. Elspeth Cook came over to see her mother and she too had little to say. Shona did not go back to the hotel, she couldn't, she was so angry with Harry, she felt as though he had let her down, as though she had not known him, which was impossible. She didn't know what to say.

At first she was glad of her decision but after a day or two she understood that her circumstances had changed so much that she missed him. She had enjoyed living at the shop before and she liked being among the people she employed but she missed his sound judgement and his reassuring presence.

She longed to be at the hotel with him or anywhere and though she missed James she missed Harry too. It was quite different but she now had nobody to talk to about her life in Paradise Lane and she had not thought how important this was to her, her father and her early life and the way that Harry had set her on to better things. She knew that the only way she and James had survived for a long time was because of the money which Harry had put by for her, what he thought of as her fair share of the payment for the work they had done over all those years.

Annabel and Ned asked her to dinner. It was not a success.

It seemed to her that there was an enormous hole in the conversation which was strange as Harry was never a talkative man these days. He had never paid her any attention while they were out or said anything of note that she could remember and it was only when Ned took her back to the shop that she thought she and Harry had gone home to the hotel and sat over the fire and talked about people, not disparagingly, just generally, and she thought how odd it was that Harry was not rude about anyone but would drive a man to take his life and she could not reconcile the two.

As it was the moment she got back she sat over the fire alone and thought back to how awful they had been about him and how defensive she had felt when he had done something indefensible.

'I can't think why you ever married him,' Caroline Atherton had said.

'It couldn't have anything to do with the fact that Harry is one of the most eligible men in the area,' Annabel said in defence and Shona had to stop herself from saying that relevant as that might be her decision had had nothing to do with such things.

'Eligible? My dear, the whole thing is practically ghoulish,' Caroline said and there were murmurs of agreement.

Ned for once had nothing to say. Annabel said privately to Shona later that that was because he was embarrassed at how much he cared for Harry and Aidan sat next to her and Lorna on her other side as though they wanted to hold her up. Lorna said that she thought Harry must have had a very good reason for what he did and other people disagreed and said that it was nothing more than greed and Shona choked over what she had thought was a very small amount of toffee pudding. It stuck to the roof of her mouth like a large stone.

All she could think was that Harry had never been greedy and that night she wished so much to go to him that she couldn't help, even though it was late, after Ned had left her, putting on her coat and walking the short distance from the market square and across Elvet Bridge, in at the front door of the County and up the stairs, without seeing anyone.

She knocked on the door twice, not very loudly, before he

opened it and there Harry stood in his shirtsleeves looking
rested and well with clear eyes and a smile. Shona wanted to
run back to the shop, she thought she had made a horrible
mistake. Had he somehow convinced himself that he had been
justified in what he had done?

He let her in, offered her coffee and since it had just been
made and there was a silver potful she agreed and he offered
her a seat and she looked around.

'So,' she said, 'Ned tells me you've pulled down the house
at Dragon's Field? Perhaps you're going to build a splendid
mansion there?'

'I don't think so,' he said.

He didn't sit down, he wandered around the room, stopping
before the fire and sipping coffee from the tiny white cup and
she thought of the other men she knew and how she would
always have chosen him for hers and that was ridiculous considering the circumstances and her grief for James. There was just
something so competent about the way that he behaved. No
wonder people were happy to put their money into his bank,
no matter what he had done.

'I doubt it too,' she said, 'mansions aren't your style.'

'Once perhaps. Not now.'

'Harry—'

He stopped her.

'Look,' he said, 'if you want a formal legal separation I will
understand. After all there's nothing between us and Aidan can
sort things out and you would get a big settlement for the
shop so that you could carry on and—' He stopped himself
there and Shona found herself saying the words she had promised herself that she would never say.

'Haven't you ever wanted me?'

'I've never wanted anybody,' he said quickly. 'I'm fine by
myself.'

'I don't think you are any more. I think you're a dreadful
liar.'

That made him laugh.

'I'd like to tempt you just once. Especially now,' she said.

'Why especially now?' he said, like an interested spectator.

'Because nobody believes in you any more.'

She got up and went to him and Harry put down the coffee cup like a challenge. He backed slightly but there was nowhere to go because there was the fire and to either side armchairs and at the front a huge sofa which she had always liked and had once or twice thought they might sit there together but they never had, they always sat in the armchairs across the fire from one another, almost like opponents.

'Go on, then,' he dared her.

'I'm not sure I know how to.'

'You must do, after years with James.'

'It wasn't the same. He loved me.'

'I love you.'

He backed a little more. She got hold of him. He could have backed even a bit more but he didn't, he stood his ground and she knew he would. His mouth was surprisingly soft and warm and trembling just a bit and his breath was a little uneven. She felt him back further and she let go of him.

'How was it?' she said looking straight into his eyes.

'I'm not sure. Could you do it again?' and after she had done so he put his face into her neck with a great sigh of relief.

'I do want you here and I'm sorry you think I've let you down.'

'I don't think you have. I don't know what to think. I don't feel about you like I felt about James but I miss you. I want to be here with you.'

It seemed that it was with a great effort that he moved, stood back and said to her, 'I think you would regret it later.'

'Why?'

He didn't answer for what seemed like a long time during which she thought he was wishing she would go so that he didn't have to answer her but she didn't, she just waited.

'Shona, look, I—' He stopped. 'I don't – I'm not—' and then he stopped again. 'I don't know how to do this.'

'Why don't you?' Her voice sounded loud to Shona, she felt as though it echoed around the room several times while he stood there and didn't look anywhere at all almost as though his eyes were closed which they weren't, she checked.

'I don't know who I am.'

From somewhere there was an echo in her head and she understood then that she had known for some time there were huge
gaps in his life and that the day she had pulled him out of the
snow was the end of something rather than the beginning and
that people did not just appear like that and lie down to die. She
had tried not to think about it too much, right from the day
she had left, but it had always been there at the back of her
consciousness and in her heaviest moments she remembered that
she had known there was something very wrong and that the only
reason he had been able to bear it was because she had saved him.

'Perhaps you don't know a lot about yourself,' she said, 'but
I know who you are.'

'You think you do?' He looked half hopefully at her.

'Oh, definitely,' she said.

There was a pause and then he said with a sort of sniff,
'When you went away it was the worst day of my life.'

Shona tried to stop the emotion from getting in the way.

'And that was saying something, eh?'

'I thought it was better really because I had and have nothing
to offer you. I should have said so when you came back but
I couldn't. I just wanted you around me, I just wanted to be
able to talk to you every day, to see you even at a distance
every day for the rest of my life. I want to be where you are,
it's the only thing that matters to me.'

'I'm not going anywhere,' she said.

'I don't want to stop you with my stupid meanderings.'

'Ah,' she said, 'you must have had a hell of an education
somewhere along the way, "meanderings", is it?'

There was another long silence and then he said, from behind
his hands which were by then covering his face, 'Oh, God,
Shona, don't leave me.'

And that was when she took him into her arms.

'I'm not going to,' she said.

Nobody said anything else, nobody did anything else.
Eventually they lay down on the sofa and he fell asleep and
she held him and was satisfied just listening to his breathing.

The following day he asked her to go to Dragon's Field with
him to see what had been done and although she was still

reluctant she couldn't deny him that though she didn't know how she was going to react when they got there.

The site had been completely cleared and only the trees in the garden were the same. The workmen were in the gardens which they were meant to be digging but they weren't, they were standing around, talking in a group, and as Harry and Shona stopped and got out of the car the head man, Richard Thompson, who was a local builder, very good and well known and Shona was glad of that, came to them, wiping the sweat from his brow although it was a cold day and he nodded at her and he said, 'I was just going to send for you. Could I talk to you by yourself?'

'Mr Thompson, this is my wife, Shona. You can say anything in front of her.'

The man paused.

'Well, if you say so. I think I should call the police. We've found something in the garden, over there.' He indicated. 'It's the remains of something. I don't know much about these things but it looks as if it's – it was a person, but a very small person, I think a child.'

Harry went so pale that Shona thought he was going to pass out but all he said was, 'I'll get the police. Tell the men to wait but they will have full wages and after they have spoken to the police they can go home.'

'I'll tell them not to say anything,' Mr Thompson offered.

Harry looked gratefully at him.

They went back to the town and to the police station and then back to the site. Shona had the feeling that Harry might try to prevent her from going with him but she hung on to his hand and he squeezed her fingers in acknowledgement of her presence and how much it meant to him that she was there.

That afternoon the police found the remains of another small body and after that they went all over the garden in case there were more. They only stopped when it was completely dark.

'You have to tell the police what you know,' she said.

He shook his head.

'You must. This is terrible and I believe you know what happened there. I think you're the only person who does.'

'I was lucky,' he said, 'I got away. They grew tired of me or I got so much older that – I didn't matter or they couldn't be bothered with me by then and they threw me out. I didn't know until recently that there had been other children – it doesn't seem as if – as if they all got out.'

'Tell me.'

So he did, he told her right from the beginning about how he had thought he was a St Clair and how it was not true and about his parents and the lack of them and the old man and then the streets and how he had survived that and finally the treatment which Jason Taylor and his friends had used, abusing children for their own gratification.

Shona was so shocked she couldn't think of anything to say. Worse still there was a knocking on the door and when they didn't answer it the knocking grew to pounding so she finally opened the door and Ned Fleming stood there, strode into the room and said instantly to Harry, 'I understand there have been some interesting goings on at Dragon's Field. How would you like to tell me about it?'

Harry looked like somebody who had just woken up. He stared at Ned as though they hadn't met before.

'It's nothing to be concerned about,' Shona said, trying to draw his fire away.

She succeeded, Ned turned around.

'I didn't expect to see you here,' he said.

Shona didn't realize what she was doing until she had stood between the two men, protecting Harry. Ned looked past her.

'I understand you have men up there guarding the site and that the police have been there for hours and they found something or somebody in the garden. Is it true?'

'If the police haven't said anything then there's nothing to say,' Harry said.

'I shall find out, you know. You might as well tell me what it is. People have a right to know.'

'People have nothing of the sort,' Harry said. 'They have a right to know about politics and football results and who has grown the best leeks in the district and about science and art but the rest of it appeals to the worst in people and they have no right whatsoever to information which is none of their concern, nor would a decent newspaper man try to make money from people's worst instincts.'

Ned looked hard at him.

'The police will tell me and word will get round, it always does.'

'Then I suggest you go back to them, I've got nothing to say.'

Ned was silent for a few moments, looked as if he was about to leave and then changed his mind.

'You've cleared the site. Can I at least ask you what you're going to do with it?'

'I'm going to build a children's hospital there.'

Shona turned around and looked hard at him and then she went to him and kissed him and she said, 'Oh, Harry, you are wonderful,' while Ned stood in silence, staring.

And from the comfort of her husband's arms she threw over her shoulder, 'You must approve of that, surely?'

'I do indeed and I shall certainly write about it but I would like the whole story.'

'Not tonight,' Harry said and he released his wife momentarily and saw his friend to the door of the suite. 'Give our best to Annabel,' he said and opened the door and urged Ned out of it and when he had gone Harry closed the door and sighed a little and stood back against it. 'People will find out.'

'Only some of it and not enough to hurt you, I think. It's over now. Come and sit down.'

He did and she sat down beside him on the sofa and drew near and kissed him.

'It will be all right,' she said and he believed her.